Ali Camacho-Febles

MCKENZIE CASSIDY is a writer, jour-
nalist, marketer, and professor living in
Fort Myers, Florida. His work has appeared in the anthology *Walk Hand in
Hand into Extinction: Stories Inspired by
True Detective*, *Flash Fiction Magazine*,
Florida Weekly, and in multiple newspapers throughout southwest Florida. He
holds an MFA from Wilkes University and
is a regular blogger for the Florida Writers
Association. *Here Lies a Father* is his first
novel. Learn more at mckenziecassidy.com.

HERE LIES
A FATHER

HERE LIES A FATHER

· A NOVEL ·

MCKENZIE CASSIDY

KAYLIE JONES BOOKS

Published by Akashic Books
©2021 Mckenzie Cassidy

ISBN: 978-1-61775-757-0
Library of Congress Control Number: 2020936138
First printing

Kaylie Jones Books
www.kayliejonesbooks.com

Akashic Books
Brooklyn, New York
Twitter: @AkashicBooks
Facebook: AkashicBooks
E-mail: info@akashicbooks.com
Website: www.akashicbooks.com

Also Available from Kaylie Jones Books

Cornelius Sky by Timothy Brandoff
The Schrödinger Girl by Laurel Brett
Starve the Vulture by Jason Carney
City Mouse by Stacey Lender
Death of a Rainmaker by Laurie Loewenstein
Unmentionables by Laurie Loewenstein
Like This Afternoon Forever by Jaime Manrique
Little Beasts by Matthew McGevna
Some Go Hungry by J. Patrick Redmond
Inconvenient Daughter by Lauren J. Sharkey
The Year of Needy Girls by Patricia A. Smith
The Love Book by Nina Solomon
The Devil's Song by Lauren Stahl
All Waiting Is Long by Barbara J. Taylor
Sing in the Morning, Cry at Night by Barbara J. Taylor
Flying Jenny by Theasa Tuohy

From Oddities/Kaylie Jones Books

Angel of the Underground by David Andreas
Foamers by Justin Kassab
Strays by Justin Kassab
We Are All Crew by Bill Landauer
The Underdog Parade by Michael Mihaley
The Kaleidoscope Sisters by Ronnie K. Stephens

For Rowan and Nora, whose own stories are about to begin . . .

Old man, look at my life
I'm a lot like you were.
—Neil Young, "Old Man"

How can I try to explain, when I do he turns away again
It's always been the same, same old story
From the moment I could talk I was ordered to listen
Now there's a way and I know that I have to go away
I know I have to go.
—Cat Stevens, "Father and Son"

FRIDAY

C HAPTER 1

WE ARRIVED IN OUR BORROWED CAR at the gates of the New Brimfield Memorial Cemetery, a series of hulking Gothic spires. The cemetery faced the vacant high school. It was a Friday in late spring and students were out early that day for a reason unknown to me. I stared at the school from our car and attempted to imagine what kind of student my father had been. Probably the opposite of what life was like for me, a fifteen-year-old sophomore with no idea what my future held. He was likely the "king of the school" in his day, with his sharp wit and natural charisma. Everybody adored him. He was a society man, although not high society. He was the type of man with a reserved barstool, a regular order of Dewar's on the rocks set on a fresh cocktail napkin when he stepped through the door, and old drinking pals waiting in line for a tirade of dirty jokes.

Until recently, I hadn't realized there were multiple versions of Thomas Daly. There was the public version, of course, the young, strong, entertaining man my mother fell in love with so many years ago, the worldly man, the intelligent leader who always had a comeback and knew the right thing to say in any situation. But there were other sides to him, ones the outside world never saw or wasn't even aware of, and ones I'd never given much thought to until today. Frustrated, miserable, introspective, a raft lost at sea, weighed down by burdens I couldn't possibly fathom. The last time I saw him alive he had transformed into a weak and brittle old man, dissolving before my eyes. I didn't know he was sick at that point, but I should've known. I only suspected that after years of not taking care of himself nature had taken its due, not that he was dying. He didn't tell a soul, but I should've known just by the look of him.

Beside the seriously brooding cemetery gate stood a short, chubby man. He wore a faded blue polo shirt that barely tucked into his belt due to a bulbous stomach. He was balding except for patches of gray hair that sprouted from the sides of his head and stood straight out, as if he'd suddenly awakened from bed and rushed out of the house without looking in a mirror. He waved at my sister Catherine and me. She rolled the car window down.

"We made it . . . finally," she said.

"Hey there," Uncle Neil responded, resting his hand on the car roof. He was alone. "Nice to see you two. I told you not to worry about time. The important thing is you're here."

"Where do we park?"

"Go ahead and use the school lot," he told Catherine. "Nobody will bother you there."

Catherine and I had driven miles from where I currently lived, a small town in upstate New York called Wellbourne, to Dad's hometown of New Brimfield. Our trip had been rife with complications. We were two hours late, having wandered curvy, poorly marked roads, unable to see past a mist left over from an early-morning thunderstorm. Having lived upstate for most of my life, except for the two-year period when Mom dragged us to Florida, I was familiar with how most back-country roads weren't marked for a driver's ease and how most directions were given by word-of-mouth. We weren't supposed to stress about being late but I could tell how much it bothered Catherine.

A gray package, about the size of a jack-in-the-box, sat in the backseat. Dad's remains. He had died two weeks earlier when the snow melted and was cremated in Albany, per Catherine's directive. The funeral director in Albany had handed Catherine his remains on the day she flew up from Florida, simple ashes in an overly priced box. I stood beside her as she received our father. I stared at the thick gold rings on the funeral director's swollen fingers. Dad's official cause of death was questionable to say the least, but one thing was certain. On his deathbed the doctor said that despite a half-century of smoking unfiltered cigarettes, Dad's lungs were the cleanest and strongest he'd ever seen. Dad never would've shared that either.

Catherine guided our orange hatchback, which we had borrowed from one of her old friends, into a vacant parking spot facing the brick high school. Between the parking lot and the cemetery gate stood a smaller building that matched the school and likely held maintenance equipment. Catherine reached into the backseat and unbuckled the box of Dad's remains. Worried that one wrong turn would send the box crashing to the floor, spewing ash all over the car's interior, we had strapped it in when the country roads grew especially bumpy. She pulled it close to her chest. The two of them had always been so close, but I guess the same thing could be said about Mom and me. Catherine thought the world of Dad, no matter what happened to him. If he had been a mass murderer, she would've defended him to her last breath.

Uncle Neil eyed the box as we approached. "Is that . . . him?"

"Yes," said Catherine.

He shivered and slipped his hands into his pockets.

Catherine was cordial with Uncle Neil, but kept her defenses up. She thanked him for working with us on such short notice to finalize our father's arrangements. There had been no real time to prepare. If anyone should have known it would've been her, but she gave no advance warning. I assumed she didn't know, but I was always the last to hear of anything involving our family. Dad's death didn't feel real to me; rather, I was watching a movie about somebody else's life. Uncle Neil didn't seem shocked about my father's death at all. He sounded more like an old classmate who hadn't run into my father since they graduated high school.

"Not a problem, he was my brother after all, even if I hadn't spoken to the son of a bitch in years," he said, chuckling. "Ian, I don't know if you remember this or not, but I spoke to you once over the phone. You must've been a little boy. Your father put you on the line. You probably don't remember."

I tried my hardest to remember, but I couldn't. Whatever part of my brain was responsible for collecting and storing memories was defective. It seemed as if—with the exception of a few worthless recollections—major chunks of my memory were missing, particularly those before the age of ten. The ones that remained were drawn from tales

Mom had recounted over and over again, and featured in the collection of photographs she hung proudly on our walls, sometimes even of strangers, to fill empty space. I desperately dredged the recesses of my mind, which seemed filled with dark mud, but came up with nothing. The truth was, I couldn't remember what Uncle Neil was talking about, but I had to answer him, so I lied. I didn't want him to feel insignificant, like his was a frivolous memory I hadn't bothered to file away.

"You know what? I remember now, yes, I do," I said, grinning. "I was standing in our kitchen, I think, the one with black-and-white tiles. Dad handed me the telephone and he was ecstatic that you had called."

Catherine peered at me. She knew I was lying. I wasn't as good as everyone else in my family and she knew my tells.

"Hmm, sure doesn't sound like him," said Neil, scratching his chin. "Usually, he was pissed whenever I called him."

"Oh," I said. "Well, that day he was in a great mood."

"I see. Well, either way, it's still nice to finally meet you in person after all these years."

Lying was wrong, I understood that, as any reasonable person would, but I also felt good about having lied to Uncle Neil. He didn't know the difference. Why make him feel bad by saying my father never mentioned a word about his brother? We had just met and I preferred keeping the peace. Uncle Neil smiled. I think it made him happy that I lied, whether he knew it or not.

"I took the liberty of picking a nice spot for Thomas," he said, pointing to a squat hill in the distance.

"Are we going there now?" asked Catherine, checking her wristwatch.

"Yes, yes. We should get things started."

Dad had been raised a Catholic, which didn't exactly support the burning of one's body for burial, yet his final arrangements were ultimately Catherine's decision. Dad had no legal will, at least not that any of us could find. He never discussed being buried or cremated, but Catherine said she couldn't stand pumping his body full of embalming chemicals for a morbid viewing and archaic ceremony. She'd rather he just return to the earth. Ashes to ashes, dust to dust, all of that. Not having met any of Dad's family members until that day, and not having any grasp of their religious leanings, I couldn't determine whether they would've disapproved of Catherine's decision. Uncle Neil didn't seem to mind, but he also could've been lying to keep the peace. By that point it didn't really matter anyway; the deed had been done.

The three of us entered the cemetery and took a paved, well-manicured path to the hilltop that would be Dad's final resting place. Our shoes got wet as we stepped onto the soggy grass and trekked up the hill. Without the headstones the landscape would have looked like a golf course, the sort of place to relax on a lazy Sunday morning. I looked out over the property. Newly installed headstones were laid out proportionately. Farther away were crumbling spires dating back hundreds of years, the names of their eternal guests barely legible. I thought about how the diggers must've toiled over spacing out the dead in such a finite space. Sooner or later the entire cemetery would be full and they'd have a problem on their hands.

Once at the hilltop, we waited patiently beside a shallow hole. Without a casket there had been no reason for the diggers to go deep. Uncle Neil scanned the horizon as a sailor would on the deck of a ship, and two blurry figures emerged through the distant cemetery gate. Two women came into focus, skipping over shallow mud puddles on their way toward us.

"We're over here!" shouted Neil, as if they hadn't seen him. He waved.

Except for us three, the cemetery was empty.

One of the women was short and stout, with a tight silver perm and a pointed nose that reminded me of Dad. She also resembled Neil, so I assumed she was a Daly. The other one was tall and thin with long, midnight-black hair and tanned, leathery skin. They followed the same route we had taken to the hilltop and when they arrived we all stood awkwardly, waiting for somebody to make the first introduction. Finally, the shorter one introduced herself as Dad's sister, Marie.

"It's so wonderful to meet you finally," said Marie. "I just wish it had been under better circumstances."

I smiled.

"We feel the same way, believe me," said Catherine. She nudged my arm.

"Yes, great to meet you too," I added. "Thanks."

As Marie spoke I glanced at the other woman, clutching her leather purse and waiting anxiously to be introduced. Her gigantic purse was black leather with gold rings. She stood a few feet back and nodded at everything we said. Marie paused briefly from her introductions and studied my face.

"You look like him, you know," she said. Everyone turned to verify, but said nothing further. "Thomas, your father. I can see him in you."

"I see that too, Marie," said the other woman, re-minding the group she was still there.

Her compliment should've made me beam with pride, but instead my stomach turned. I didn't want them to see the look of disgust on my face, so I stared at every-one's shoes. Uncle Neil wore scuffed penny loafers, Ma-rie stood flat-footed in white walking sneakers, and the other woman leaned to the side in black high-heel ankle boots. I couldn't explain why I reacted the way I did to Marie's observation, yet once the day was over I'd push the thought out of my mind forever.

"Oh, how rude of me," said Marie. "This is Carla."

The dark-haired stranger, Carla, stepped forward and shook our hands loosely with her two longest fingers and thumb.

"Nice to meet you," said Catherine. With a pointed glance, she demanded that Marie explain why this strange woman was present at our father's funeral. Not being able to wait any longer, she started fishing for answers. "So, Carla, are you a member of the family or a friend or . . . ?"

"Not exactly," Marie answered casually. "Carla is Thomas's ex-wife."

Catherine's face turned crimson, she scrunched it up questioningly, and she tipped her head to one side. "I'm sorry, I misheard you."

"Thomas, your father," said Marie, slowly. "Carla was his first wife."

Catherine searched desperately for the truth in each of the faces gathered around Dad's grave. I looked up to the sky, imagining I was anyplace else but in that ceme-tery. Back when I used to play outfield for the Wellbourne junior baseball team, I'd place my leather glove over my face like a mask and watch the game unfold through the stitch holes. The crowd in the bleachers used to scream at me when I missed a pop fly or struck out at bat, but I persisted because I wanted so badly to be a part of something, to make friends with the other players. I just couldn't focus long enough to learn the fundamentals of the game. Eventually I quit the team.

"His first wife?" repeated Catherine. She had heard what Marie had said, but she wanted to give her mind time to process.

"His first wife," said Marie.

Tears filled Carla's eyes. She blinked and they streamed down her leathery cheeks, leaving a moist trail of orange spray tan. "I'm so sorry," she said, sobbing. "I was afraid this was going to happen."

"Afraid *what* was going to happen?" asked Catherine defensively.

"I was afraid you two wouldn't have known about his other marriages. That he never told you. I shouldn't have come. I'm so, so sorry." Carla slung her oversized purse back over her shoulder and turned to leave.

"Stop. Stop. Don't be crazy," said Marie. She put her hand on Carla's back. "You have as much a right as anyone else to be here. You were married to the man, for Christ's sake."

"Thank you," said Carla, sniffing. "But . . . this just isn't appropriate."

"You got that right," said Catherine.

Carla retrieved a balled-up tissue from her purse and dabbed her tears.

Marie turned to Catherine and me, and I could tell

she was concerned. "Are you telling me your parents never mentioned any of this?" she asked.

"Other marriages?" said Catherine in a strained voice. She was an English major in college and knew the difference between plural and singular. "No. Absolutely not."

"Marriages. Yes. Your father had a few," said Marie, smirking.

Not long after Marie dropped this bomb, Carla also dropped the shy-and-withdrawn act. "Thomas and I had two children together, Mark and Ashley, before he left me. They're much older than you, as you'd probably guess, and they have lives of their own now, but they're your half siblings."

Marie clearly had no idea of how this shocking news would plow through our psyches, leaving craters the size of volcanoes. Speaking openly about our personal lives didn't come easy for my family. Before leaving town Mom and Catherine had specifically told me not to give them an inch, to keep my eyes and ears open about whether any of *those backwoods kooks* were trying to profit from Dad's death. If there had been money floating around, Mom said, we'd better figure out if they'd fight over it or not. Money was funny business in my family; we refused to admit we cared about it, but there was never a time when it wasn't the topic of conversation.

"Is this a prank?" asked Catherine, struggling to crack a smile to show she was in on the joke. Considering Dad's dark humor, it was fair to assume he got it from his family. "My father did *not* have other families or other children, and if this is a joke I'd appreciate it if you all stopped carrying on with it. It's not the time or place."

Marie, unruffled, responded calmly to Catherine's

outburst: "I'm sorry, sweetie. I wish it was a joke."

Catherine and Mom never included me in the important matters of the Daly family. As if I'd been bestowed a nonessential status, it wasn't important for me to know what was happening or why they had made certain choices over the years. They excluded me because they wanted to protect me from the harsh realities of this world. How could I fault them for that? But now I was hearing something live, at the same time as Catherine, and we were left to figure out whether it was true. Dad's family had no reason to lie, nothing to gain.

If it were true, and at that moment I thought it might be, it meant Dad had lied to me—to everyone—for years.

"Hey, these confessions are great and all, but don't forget we're all here for a funeral," said Neil. "Let's get on with it and we can all catch up later."

"I agree," said Marie. "We have all of the time in the world."

"Yes. Fine. Let's just do it already," said Catherine. She gently placed Dad's box, which she had been hoarding since we had arrived, at the bottom of the shallow hole.

Carla reached inside her behemoth purse and pulled out a handful of roses like a Las Vegas magician. She told us she'd bought them fresh at a grocery store on the way to the cemetery. She handed one to each of us. I remembered how Mom hated roses because they reminded her of funerals, but Dad bought them for her every Valentine's Day regardless. As much as she complained, he kept buying them. He never listened, she said. I wondered if he bought roses for every woman?

Uncle Neil explained that the diggers would fill the

hole properly that evening, but the dirt inside of the white buckets could be ceremoniously spread across the top of Dad's box. He reached into one bucket and pulled up a handful of dirt, sprinkling it on the box like he was seasoning a stew. He passed the bucket around and each of us took our share. We also dropped the roses onto the uneven mounds, which had transformed into mud upon hitting the wet ground. I thought it all defeated the purpose of buying fresh flowers. Some of the soil stuck to my hands, so I wiped them across the wet blades of grass by my feet.

"I think that about does it," said Neil.

"Should we say something?" asked Marie, her hands folded and resting on her stomach.

"Like what? I'm not a goddamn priest," he said.

"No, Neil, she's right," said Carla. "I can say something if—"

"No, that's quite all right, Carla," Catherine blurted. She could barely speak through a clenched jaw. "You've done quite enough. He was my father, so I can take it from here."

We all bowed our heads.

"We are gathered here on this peaceful and beautiful hilltop today, somewhat overcast, to say goodbye to Thomas Daly. He was a good man. He cared deeply about his family, friends, and the community in which he lived. Anyone who had the good fortune of spending time with him loved him. He will be greatly missed and I only wish I could do more to help celebrate his tremendous life. Amen."

A cold breeze blew a pile of soggy leaves down the hill. We took a moment of silence, yet my mind was screaming. Thoughts of death bounced across the empty spaces. I had only faced it one other time in my life, when my grandfather passed away and I was too young to understand. My younger cousin and I had climbed up to the lid of his coffin to wake him up from his nap, something I had done a hundred times before. I tried to visualize the day of my maternal grandfather's funeral too, but like most of my memories, they were murky and disjointed. I remembered how people were packed elbow-to-elbow, all in black, sobbing and sharing stories about him. He had a full wake with cold cuts and my grandmother sat in the living room to greet the people who came to pay their respects.

In the end, Dad's funeral was five strangers standing awkwardly around a two-foot-by-two-foot hole, tossing handfuls of dirt into an unmarked grave with grocery store roses. I decided on that hilltop, staring at his partially filled resting place, that when I died I wanted hundreds of people at my funeral—a great party where everyone shared their fond memories of me, and stayed late into the night because they couldn't stand to let me go. I didn't want to die alone.

CHAPTER 2

EACH OF US WANTED TO PAY OUR RESPECTS, yet none of us wanted to overstay. Funerals weren't for the dead anyway. They gave those left behind a chance to grieve and tie up loose ends. I watched Catherine as she delivered her impromptu sermon. Her black hair, in sharp contrast with her pale skin, fell down the sides of her pronounced cheekbones. As brother and sister we were both pale and turned red like boiled lobsters on the beach, which was another reason I never understood why our family moved to Florida for two years and then unexpectedly came home in the middle of the school year, about six months earlier. We never finished what we started. People said Catherine and I looked alike because we both had full cheeks and slightly pointed noses that appeared to slide down our foreheads. And we both had big Irish chins. My father, Thomas Daly, was of full Irish descent—at least that's what he told us—while Mom's family was mostly German or English. Her name was Helen.

We all had loose ends to tie up. Catherine needed to say goodbye to her beloved father, Marie and Neil to their estranged brother, and our esteemed guest Carla a farewell to her old flame, if in fact there was any truth to her story. I'd come to do what any good son did when his father died, yet none of it was going how I'd expected. Once Carla opened her mouth about Dad's other alleged marriages, I felt like everything was in a tailspin. Regardless of whether her story was true or not, it consumed my thoughts. The truth didn't matter as much as the way a story made you feel, and fate had given me a chance to maybe learn something real about my father, something he never would've told me himself. I was apprehensive about not liking what I'd potentially learn, nervous about ripping off the lid and being haunted by what I'd find inside.

Catherine tossed the final handful of dirt into Dad's shallow grave. She brushed her hands together and excess granules fell from her fingers. She looked out over the cemetery grounds. At first, I assumed she was surveying the property where our father would spend his eternity at rest, but instead I could now tell she was orchestrating our speedy departure.

"I appreciate you all meeting us here today, but I think it's time we left," she said.

"Oh, no, really? So soon?" said Marie.

We had barely spent half an hour at the cemetery, which felt unfulfilling after the excessive time it took us to drive across the state.

"I'm sorry, but we have plans with our family."

"But . . . we made plans," Marie said desperately. "Didn't Neil tell you? Neil, you said you—"

"Yes, Marie," Neil exhaled, hot steam leaving his exhaust pipe of a mouth. "I told them about it this morning, Marie."

"What plans?" I asked.

Earlier that day we had taken a break from driving so

Catherine could use a pay phone beside a peculiar-looking gas station. Many of the pumps were out of order and had yellow bags covering them. The building had been two stories, somebody's get-rich-quick scheme, the kind Dad always sought out. Whoever owned it must've lived upstairs, which reminded me of when we were kids and Dad proposed we move above a bar he wanted to buy in Wellbourne. We toured the apartment to make him feel better, a musty place with carpets sticky from triple sec and cherry juice, and thin walls that failed to muffle the loud clinking of bottles and the scraping of wooden barstools downstairs. Mom said no. *Hell no*, in fact. They fought and argued over it for weeks yet we never moved in. Months later the building mysteriously burned to the ground, but that was pure coincidence.

Nearly three songs had played on the radio rotation before Catherine returned from using the phone. Smashing Pumpkins. The Gin Blossoms. Radiohead. Once back in the car she had cleverly avoided telling me who was on the line. *Don't worry about it,* she had said. One of my father's favorite sayings, one he often repeated to my mother to put her at ease when she was nervous about the state of things. *Don't worry about it.* The line never accomplished what it intended, of course. Catherine had clearly been on the phone with Uncle Neil, most likely to update him on our progress, and for some reason she decided not to share the postfuneral plans with me. I knew that Catherine had a flight back to Florida either Monday or Tuesday, so she may've been in a hurry to get back, but I had no immediate plans.

"You two drove so far and we thought you could stay the night and spend some more time with us," said Marie.

Carla stepped forward. "That's a fabulous idea, Marie." She avoided eye contact with Catherine as she spoke.

"I don't know," Catherine said. "I'm sorry about all this, but we're so behind already, getting lost and all, and if we don't leave now we'll be driving back in the dark. I just don't want to get lost again."

Uncle Neil cocked an eyebrow at Catherine. "Your car has headlights, doesn't it?"

"Well, yes, of course, but I just don't want to get lost again. We don't know these roads very well. Plus, our mother is expecting us home tonight."

The reference to my mother piqued Carla's interest. "Could you call her from Marie's house? I'd love to meet her officially, even if it's over the phone."

"Fantastic idea, Carla," said Marie, smiling as if they had rehearsed the conversation beforehand.

"No. We can't," said Catherine. "As I said, we have to go. Thanks and all, but goodbye."

As far as Catherine was concerned, *the others* didn't exist. There was no reason to stick around and learn about their inconsequential lives. She knew our father particularly well, arguably better than anyone else, and she didn't want his memory to be tarnished. I had a hard time believing Carla's claim as well, that strange children with *my* father's looks and quirks were out walking, talking, and carrying on lives of their own. I couldn't stop thinking about how it all sounded like a bad episode of *The Twilight Zone*. I had friends in school whose parents were divorced and later remarried into other families with children, but I had never heard of anything quite like this.

Catherine hooked her arm in mine and subtly dragged me down the hill like a child.

"Wait a second, Catherine," I said as we stepped onto the path that led to the front gate. "If we're already here, wouldn't it be easier to stay?"

"Not now," she hissed.

Not wanting to be rude, I waved back at the group as we neared the gate. Catherine and I circled the brick maintenance building and arrived back at our parked orange hatchback. Her hands were trembling as she struggled to slide the key into the door, and she only started to vent once we were safely inside.

"Holy shit!" she shouted, turning the ignition so hard that the car's engine made a grinding noise. "I knew it wasn't going to be as easy as I thought, that somebody would show up peddling bullshit."

"Are we really leaving?"

"Hell yes we are. Did you actually think we'd stay here for the weekend?" She adjusted the rearview mirror and started backing the car out.

"I don't know," I said. "It just seems—"

"That's enough, Ian!" she shouted. "We need to get the hell out of here and that's it." She craned her head out the window to ensure we had enough room to pull out. "And not a word of this to Mom."

The parking lot was narrow and Catherine needed to do a U-turn. She rode the edge of the pavement as we circled and tore past the cemetery gate. Neil, Marie, and Carla had reached the parking lot. They halfheartedly nodded at me as we passed and I returned the gesture through the passenger window. Our wheels skidded a bit and Catherine accelerated harder. We left the old high school in a blur, across the parking lot, and spotted the Main Street intersection. From there we'd backtrack through the poorly marked country roads and merge onto the highway toward Wellbourne. Within a few hours we'd be home and nothing would stand in our way, but then our tire burst and the car leaned heavily to one side. Catherine slammed on the brakes.

"What the hell?" she said, opening her door to investigate.

I got out as well. Not that I knew anything about cars, but I thought it was the right thing to do. Catherine left the engine running and hot exhaust floated around the car like fog, a rank odor reminding me of waiting for an order at a drive-thru. We both peered under the driver's-side door. Only rubber shards remained where our tire used to be. Large hunks of black rubber were scattered behind us, a path which led a concerned-looking Uncle Neil straight our way.

"Shit, shit, shit," Catherine said, clenching her jaw as she saw him approach. "Let me do the talking. Whatever happens, we aren't staying!"

"Hey! Are you two all right? I heard a loud bang. Is everyone okay?" called out Neil.

Catherine waved dismissively. "It's fine, we're just fine, don't worry about us."

In no time he was standing beside us, out of breath and inspecting the car like old know-it-all men do. He wasn't in very good physical shape. He put a hand on the car hood, groaned, and eased himself onto one knee to study the damage.

"Yup, yup, the tire is blown. If it was just a leak you could've patched it up and driven home by now, but you'll be needing a brand-new tire," he said.

"I can certainly see that," Catherine said. "We'll be

fine, Neil, don't let us keep you, if you have someplace else to be. Just tell me where we can go for a new tire."

"Not safe to drive on the donut, not safe at all. Do you have some kind of roadside service?"

Catherine ignored him.

"There's only one place in town. Chuck's Tires," he said, looking at his black digital watch, waterproof up to eight hundred meters. "But Chuck closes at five and it's quarter till. You'll have to wait until the morning."

"Seriously? There's no place else that sells tires?"

"Not anywhere within fifty square miles. You'll have to stay the night."

Catherine punted a hunk of rubber across the road into the grass. She relocated to the curb, pondering what to do next.

Uncle Neil decided to change his tack and he turned toward me. "Ian, listen, you two can stay the night. I know your sister has her heart set on getting back to Wellbourne tonight, but I don't think that's going to happen." He talked past Catherine as if she wasn't there. "You two can get that tire changed tomorrow morning and be on your way."

Catherine glared at me in a panic because the decision was now in my hands. She had likely concocted an elaborate story about why the answer had to be no, but the choice was no longer hers. I wanted to tell her we had no choice, but nothing upset her more than not getting her own way. I couldn't tell for sure, because she stood by the curb, but she appeared to be mouthing *No* to me. I shrugged.

"Sure, we'd be happy to stay," I said, beaming.

Catherine dropped her face into her hands. She'd be

furious at me, but we had no choice. I understood her side, I really did.

CHAPTER 3

CATHERINE WATCHED AS NEIL AND I carefully pushed the orange hatchback into a parking space facing the high school's main entrance. She sighed and shifted her weight from one hip to the other, crossing her arms and then dropping them to her sides. Neil and I ripped off the extra hunks of rubber from the wheel well, revealing the car's skeletal metallic undercarriage. Using a rather small jack we attached the donut tire to keep the car as level as possible. In the meantime it would sit alone in the lot, which neither of us were too worried about in a small town like New Brimfield. Once the car situation was settled, we followed Uncle Neil.

He drove a Cadillac. Right on the cusp of being considered an antique, the Cadillac was aged but didn't possess the hip vintage style so beloved by car enthusiasts. He shuffled us over and unlocked the front door with a long silver key. The car had no power locks and he awkwardly bent over the passenger seat and pulled up the lock knob, breathing heavily and grunting with each movement. The Cadillac was dark purple with a white rubber top—although it wasn't a convertible—and the rims were twisted shiny spokes like a brand-new bicycle. I wanted to improve Catherine's mood so I gave her the front seat, yanking the lever near the floor and pushing the seat forward so I could squeeze myself into the back. Catherine sat down and immediately pulled the seat belt across her chest and clicked it into the buckle. I struggled to find the belts in the back. There were no shoulder straps and the buckles had slipped down the cushion cracks long ago.

Once Uncle Neil climbed into the driver's seat, the Cadillac dropped about a foot and released a metallic groan. He breathed a sigh of relief also, one he'd been holding inside to rally his robust midsection around the steering wheel. The car smelled stale too, like cigarette smoke. I glanced at the dashboard, at the ashtray more specifically, and saw that the small plastic container with a reflective facade of stainless steel was clean and untouched. Smoking in the car didn't bother me much. There wasn't a time I rode in the car when my parents didn't have cigarettes hanging out of their mouths. The reek of smoke stuck to everything we owned, from the clothes on our backs to the bags we carried to school, and our walls always turned yellow from the burning nicotine.

Uncle Neil drove through the side of town Catherine and I hadn't seen when we first arrived. The nicer houses were near the center of New Brimfield. The neighborhoods reminded me of a cul-de-sac on which my family had once lived. A cul-de-sac was a fancy way of saying dead end. Most of our neighbors were doctors and lawyers—professionals—and I'm certain we were the only ones on the block who didn't own our house. None of them knew that, of course. Mom kept the house up, planted fresh flowers under the windowsills and mowed our well-fertilized, emerald-green yard. During the holidays, like Christmas or the Fourth of July, Mom sent Catherine and me out with boxes of fudge for the neighbors, or miniature American flags to stick in their front yards. No one had any idea we didn't belong in that neighborhood, and they certainly didn't know we barely scrounged up enough money each month to pay rent and utilities. Everything was an act, but for a time, it worked.

Mom said she had no interest in owning a home because she didn't want to be held down in one place for too long. Her only valued possessions were pictures. She was compelled to always document the good times. Our walls were covered in picture frames of all shapes and sizes, easy to swap out or strike down, based on her mood or fancy. Sometimes she even hung a frame with the stock photo to further an aesthetic only she had in mind. There were pictures she only put out when certain people visited, like her mother, and others she replaced periodically to conceal outdated hairstyles or months when she had put on unexpected weight. For her, the placement of pictures was an art of personal expression, and they each told a story, her story. As the years passed I noticed fewer pictures with Dad. I didn't know why he had been excluded, but a simple answer would've been that he wasn't around as much.

Uncle Neil drove under two flashing red lights on Main Street and took a sharp right onto a dirt road. Thick forests surrounded the car on both sides. Only the occasional gravel driveway leading to cabins and camping pavilions indicated that anyone else lived in the area. I pushed open the backseat window about six inches, as far as it would go, and breathed in the fresh country air. I caught a whiff of saturated soil, pungent pine needles.

We sat quietly and I grew queasy, either from stress or the bumpy road. I took a series of deep breaths, which seemed to help. An uncle I'd just met was driving me to the home of an aunt I never knew existed, to meet an estranged family who was likely as uninterested in me as my sister Catherine was in them. I was journeying into uncharted territory and Catherine was a tether to the only reality I'd ever known. The next two days would be daunting for sure, but something about the situation felt right.

When Neil slowed the Cadillac and began turning into a driveway, I sat up and pressed myself against the glass to take a good look. Marie's house was long and narrow, a manufactured home—not a trailer, exactly—painted a drab shade of gray. The front patio was a later addition, supported by a pile of cinder blocks and covered with a makeshift roof of corrugated tin. The windows were smaller than in typical houses and overlooked patches of dead grass. If not for the white smoke that seeped from the stovepipe chimney and a car parked out front, I would've thought it abandoned. We stepped across a muddy driveway and our shoes sank into the bog. I'd have to take mine off to avoid tracking mud across Marie's house, but my socks felt wet so I'd have to change them too. That's when I suddenly realized that Catherine and I had no change of clothes, not even a toothbrush. We had never expected to stay the night.

Neil stepped onto the porch, opened the screen door, and knocked. Marie answered, smiling, and ushered us inside, which was surprisingly warm and pleasant despite its rough exterior. The living room had a deep red shag carpet and she asked us to sit down on her blue sectional couch. She even pulled a wooden lever on the side so I could recline and raise my feet.

"Take a load off, everyone," she said, busying herself in the kitchen. "I'm going to fix some coffee."

Oak-colored cabinets lined one side of her kitchen while the adjacent wall was plastered in blue-and-white wallpaper with floral designs. She didn't have as many pictures in her house as Mom did—in fact, no one did—but I saw one of a young man, his wife, and a baby. I didn't want to ask her because it was none of my business, but I assumed they were her family. Photographs are often unreliable, though. They only capture a moment in time, seldom the truth. Mom toiled over every picture hanging on our walls. They told a story and were displayed in a very specific way. Her personal favorites were from her own happy childhood in Fairfall Valley, a tiny hamlet in upstate New York, even smaller than Wellbourne.

There was no better place in the entire world to grow up, she said. I stewed with jealousy when she described her youth to me and I never stopped to wonder if that was the reaction she had intended. We'd never have it as good as she had—end of story. Her family was poor, yes, but happy. She left town at nineteen for a job waiting tables in Wellbourne, in her own words, "to get away from *your* grandmother." That's when she met my father, Thomas Daly, a well-respected manager of the community's only hotel. He served on numerous civic and nonprofit boards. Some people said he could've run for mayor and won.

Catherine and I spent most of our summers in Fairfall Valley. Mom dropped us off with my Aunt Cynthia, who lived next door to my grandmother. Our stays with Aunt Cynthia felt like days or weeks, but I couldn't recall precisely. We caught rainbow trout from creeks nearby; they glistened and writhed in our hands. We had to cut our fishing lines with curved shears when snapping turtles attached to the lure. The snapping turtles were also the reason we didn't go swimming. On breezy afternoons we ran through rows of cornstalks, hot streaks of sunshine boring through the gaps in the leaves, until giant bumblebees stung our legs and cool mud was the only remedy to soothe the pain.

As I stood looking around Marie's home, I remembered how Mom, Catherine, and I celebrated our birthdays and attended summer picnics in Fairfall Valley, but Dad never came. He didn't have time, with his heavy work schedule. He worked such long, erratic hours. Those days were tough for Mom, but she never asked for help from anybody. She was too proud. She did what she needed to do to survive. I remembered, once, she told me she'd scrubbed toilets when Dad had to find jobs elsewhere and wasn't sending any money. That was when he had started taking jobs all over the state, living in staff dormitories for months at a time, rather than commuting back and forth, to save on gas. It was hard for us, but he always came back. Always. I respected him for being such a hard worker and provider, but it had been strange how his growing absence from the family was never questioned.

Marie finally stepped out of the kitchen holding three mismatched coffee mugs. On the coffee table she set down a dented tin of sugar, a couple of soap-spotted spoons, and a white porcelain dairy cow full of fresh cream. She also set out some leftovers, trail mix, and bags of potato chips, but no one was hungry. The mug I lifted was white and brown, its handle the thick head of a Great Dane. I only added a few drops of creamer into my coffee and a quarter-spoon of sugar. Catherine sat beside me on the couch, her purse occupying the space between us. Neil kept his coffee black and leaned against the wall jutting into the living room. I realized that the only person missing was Carla. I wondered if she was avoiding us.

Marie sat in a vacant recliner, took a big sip of her steaming black coffee, her hands wrapped around the mug, and rocked herself with a smile. "This is simply wonderful," she said, looking around the dim room. "For the longest time I asked Thomas to let us all meet, but it just never seemed to work out. And look at us now!"

"Yes, look at us now," repeated Catherine vacantly.

"How has your mother been doing through all of this?"

"It's been rough on her," I said. "I think that's why she chose not to come with us."

For any wife, losing a man with whom she'd spent a quarter of her life would be crushing. Such a reaction made perfect sense. While speaking to Marie, I had simply communicated how I felt my mother was most likely feeling, how any wife would feel in this situation. I didn't know if that was the true reason Mom stayed home, and besides, she didn't share her thoughts with me. I had been with her the day Dad died, or at least the day when the news was delivered to us, and she hadn't seemed very upset. She may have been in complete shock.

"When you see her, please give her my condolences," Marie said. "Thomas's former relationships were shaky to say the least, but people change and it sounds as if, with your mother, he found the person who was meant for him."

"That's not entirely accurate," interrupted Catherine. "Before he passed, my father was alone in Albany. My mother got the ridiculous idea in her head to move us all down to Florida, but she got bored again after two years. She came back with Ian first, about six months ago, and my father never rejoined them. They were separated."

I laughed nervously.

Catherine obviously hadn't understood the situation. Mom and I had returned to Wellbourne first so she could arrange for a new job and place to live. The next step of the plan was for Dad to join us when he was ready, after he had resigned and settled any debts in Florida. Catherine knew, as well as Mom and I, that he was in Albany making the important connections needed to secure a job. His absence was no different than the summers he spent working at the resorts on the other side of the state. Sooner or later he always came back.

"Really? Separated?" Marie asked, stunned from the revelation.

"Is it that surprising, Marie?" said Neil, taking a sip from the coffee he'd been balancing on his potbelly throughout the conversation. "The man was married twice before."

"Tragic nonetheless, I'm sorry to hear that."

"Honestly, though," I chimed in, "I wouldn't say separated. They weren't living in the same house, but it wasn't like they were getting a divorce. A lot of families live apart, especially if their jobs are in different places. It's not like it used to be, you know. It's not the 1950s anymore."

The room fell silent, as if someone had just made an offensive remark, and everyone avoided eye contact with me. They took sips of their steaming coffees instead.

"So, Ian, tell us about your life," Marie finally said. "What do you like to do for fun?"

"Nothing, really."

"Oh, that's not true. A boy your age, you must have a million interests and hobbies. Video games, sports, girls?" She chuckled. "Do you play any sports at school?"

I hated when people asked if I played sports. Blood pumped like a bass drum through my jaw. This tingling warmth crept up the surface of my face and I felt like shaking. Old men were the worst when they asked me about sports. They stared at me in disbelief when I said I didn't have a favorite team and never watched any games, like I was a freak or a leper, like there was nothing more that could be done for me. I was a lost cause; better to be left alone. They were members of an exclusive club and I'd never be invited. I could only watch from a distance, through the chain-link fence.

Dad and I never watched sports together or discussed teams. I think he was so busy with work he didn't want to disappoint me by promising something he couldn't de-liver. Mom said sports were for knuckle draggers anyway, a big waste of time, so my interests unfolded elsewhere. Since we'd come back from Florida I had been training regularly at an amateur boxing gym in Wellbourne. The workouts were intense and grueling, but I looked forward to the agony. I never talked about it because I didn't want anyone to roll their eyes at my ridiculousness or think I came from a bad family. Besides, the idea of me fighting was laughable. Troubled boys with criminal records and violent fathers went into boxing, not docile, ineffectual teenagers like me.

I had waited too long to answer Marie's question and she regarded me with concern. Given the extraordinary circumstances that brought us to New Brimfield in the first place, I decided to break normal protocol and provide a straightforward, honest answer to her. I'd never see her again anyway.

"I've been going to an amateur boxing gym," I said. Air escaped my mouth rapidly like I had been holding my breath.

Marie set her coffee mug down on the coffee table, a Las Vegas mug with a giant set of colorful dice printed on one side, and she smiled. "That is so fascinating," she said. "What made you decide to start doing that?"

"Nothing, really. I don't go much," I said, trying to downplay it.

"Is that where you got the black eye?"

I reacted without thinking, bringing my hand up to my face. "Oh, it's still noticeable?"

"Well, faintly really, but I can see where you had one recently. Did you have a fight recently or something?"

I stammered and tried to think of an excuse. "Well, no, of course not. I'm not very serious about it. But, sort of, I mean, it was from all that stuff, so, yes."

She looked confused.

"It's not a big deal," I said. I wasn't ready to tell her the real story behind my black eye. "I only do it once in a while. Not every day or anything. It's not a big deal."

Before my first night at the Wellbourne Boxing Club I'd been carrying the flyer in my pocket for two weeks straight. I couldn't initially muster the courage to go. The gym was housed in the back of an office building at the

What a strange question—what other reason would I have for entering?

Bud Johnson and I were about the same size, but his cheeks were flushed and his round belly filled his faded sweatshirt. His gray hair was carefully barbered and brushed to one side. His most pronounced feature was the flatness of his nose, like someone had used a roller on it, and I realized it was from years of getting punched in the face.

"Call me Bud, by the way. For tonight, just do whatever you see everyone else doing until you start to pick up the basics. There is always one thing I tell new recruits, whether they last one night or one year, and that is: you get out of it only what you put in. If you're prepared to work hard, you'll see the fruits of your labor. If not, then you only have yourself to blame."

I nodded in understanding, but really I had no idea what he was talking about.

Inside the gym there were four heavy leather bags covered with gray duct tape, hanging from long chains attached to metal beams in the ceiling. They looked like giant, dusty cocoons. The gym was narrow. A homemade boxing ring, four feet high with three wooden steps, fit snug in the far corner. Beside the ring was a rickety card table full of musty gear: gloves, headgear, jump ropes, and pads that you put on like underwear to protect your groin. Some of the gear was decades old.

We started stretching and warming up. I saw my breath as I did jumping jacks. Bud could tell I was nervous and he smiled encouragingly. I wore a ratty San Francisco 49ers T-shirt, even though I didn't watch football, and hoped he wouldn't ask me if they were my favorite team because I'd have to lie. Below the waist I sported a pair of baggy, worn-out sweatpants that looked like pantaloons. My clothes had been graciously donated secondhand from my cousins in Fairfall Valley, including a pair of old soccer sneakers to cushion my feet. Mom insisted everything was as good as new and that we didn't have the money to purchase new anyway.

Bud asked me whether I had hand wraps or a mouth guard. I shook my head.

"I didn't think so, but we have some extra just in case," he said, pulling a dusty cardboard box from under the ring and slamming it down on the tabletop.

He dug around inside the box for a moment and pulled out two bright-yellow hunks of cloth. He unrolled them like toilet paper and they reached the other end of the gym. He lifted my left arm, which had been resting on my side, to begin rolling the cloth across my wrist and palm. I had to spread my fingers out wide as he circled the cloth over and over so it was snug but not too tight. He systematically wrapped it around my wrist, over my thumb, and around my knuckles until a thick padding covered my hands.

"Always wear these when you train," he said. "They protect your hands from being broken or sprained. You won't have to worry about those injuries as much once you get the proper form down, but wear the wraps anyway to be safe. They're important. Got it?"

I nodded blankly.

He placed two swollen gloves on my wrapped hands and led me to a dangling red heavy bag. I tried to recall whether I had consented to the class in the first place, but now it was too late. He led me around the room like a timid puppy.

"The only thing you need to worry about right now is the jab," he said.

"The what?" I asked quietly so the two teenagers wouldn't hear me.

Bud brought his fists to his cheeks and threw a straight left into the air. "Like this. Keep your hands up at all times and throw your left straight into the bag. Master that and we'll go over more later."

"Just this one punch?" I asked.

"That's it," he said. "One step at a time."

Practicing one punch at a time didn't seem difficult. When I tried baseball or football they expected you to be the best on the first day, but now I got to learn and master techniques step-by-step. I swung my arms around like a propeller to loosen my shoulders before I started throwing punches. Bud set a digital timer for three minutes and stepped into the ring with one of the teenagers, an Italian boy, to work the mitts. Bud wore pads over his hands so the boy could focus on sharpening his skills on smaller targets.

There seemed to be an unspoken rule that you didn't get to do the mitts until you showed enough promise not to waste Bud's time. It was only my first day and I didn't want to waste his time. I so badly wanted to be hitting those pads. I wanted to be a part of it all. The bell rang and the Italian boy shuffled up to Bud, started bobbing, weaving, and striking the mitts like it was choreographed, but it wasn't. Seeing Bud work with the Italian boy inspired me and I threw a couple of feeble lefts, the first of which resembled someone swatting a fly, and the next bending my wrist the wrong way on impact. I grunted in pain and looked around to make sure nobody had seen me.

The round ended and Bud stepped outside into the parking lot. The Italian boy came down too, glistening, and undid his gloves with his teeth. He stood next to me like a person who wants to start a conversation but can't think of what to say.

"Hey," he said after a moment, holding out his hand. He wore a black tank top showing off his large shoulders. His biceps looked like someone had shoved baseballs under his skin.

"Hey, how's it going?" I took his hand, damp with sweat. "Where did Bud go?"

"Oh, he went out for a smoke. Funny, isn't it? A boxing coach who rides us about healthy choices, but grabs two smoke breaks a night. Good job on the bag tonight."

I didn't know why he said that. Either he was being sarcastic or he didn't want to crush my feelings on the first day. But the longer I studied his face the more I realized he was genuine. He didn't seem like the kind of guy who was afraid to declare his true feelings on any subject. If only I had been like him, instead of some clumsy, worthless liar. He was the kind of guy I would've despised for being so good-looking and charming. My initial assumption was that he treated everyone like garbage, but I was wrong. I would come to learn that he didn't care what anyone thought about him and he wasn't an ass. I'd never met anyone like him before.

local fairgrounds, vacant year round until the traveling
carnival came to town each summer. Crumpled pieces of
wax paper, remnants of giant pretzels, and fried dough
rolled across the grounds like tumbleweeds. A large
wooden grandstand was occasionally used for cattle auc-
tions, rodeos, and demolition derbies, but otherwise it
sat like a creepy ghost town all year long. The sun had
set when I first arrived by foot, but an eerie purple and
orange glow made the clouds resemble the sky of some
faraway planet.

I stood in front of the entrance and weighed my options.

I wasn't big enough. I wasn't strong enough. I wasn't
tough enough. I wasn't coordinated or athletic enough. I
had quit everything I'd ever started. I didn't know anyone at the gym. They would all laugh at me. Everyone at
school would make fun of me when they heard about it. I
would break my nose, and Mom would get spooked and
ban me from leaving the house ever again. But something
in me, maybe a sense of destiny or adventure, forced my
hand to reach for the door. There had always been an
instinctual side to me, yearning to be dangerous and un-
characteristic, yet I had learned to bury it deep.

I took a breath, exhaled, and pulled open the gym
door, plowing a thin pile of snow flurries to the side of the
walkway. I couldn't open it all the way, on account of it
being wooden, warped, and old, but I managed to squeeze
myself inside and saw three people standing around, two
teenagers and an old man. They looked bewildered and I
realized they probably didn't get many new visitors.

The old man turned as he heard the creaking of the
door. He smiled. "Hello," he said, stepping up to me. "My
name's Bud Johnson. Are you here for the club?"

C HAPTER 4

I STARED AT MARIE AS SHE SIPPED HER COFFEE. I still hadn't made up my mind about Carla's story. I wanted to ask if it was all a lie, but my thoughts were conflicted. Although I was in the thick of it, I still didn't give myself permission to rock the boat. Questioning my own world didn't feel natural, and I was terrified of ripping the bandage off old wounds. Staying silent was much easier.

I didn't doubt that a relationship of one sort or another had existed between Carla and Dad when they were younger, especially because of how emotional she was at his burial, yet whether it was to the extent she described was questionable. Either way, I felt it was unhealthy for her to have held on this long. The day some girl dumped me, which was bound to happen, I'd vanish from her life completely. Never would I permit it to be public knowledge that I was still pining for her, because it was nobody's business. But maybe Carla couldn't handle seeing Dad move on to a better woman like my mother, so she concocted a bogus story about bearing his illegitimate children to rip our lives apart? Anything was possible at that point.

The truth was, women loved Dad, which I never understood because he wasn't particularly attractive.

I assumed it was his confidence, his biting sense of humor, and the ability to appear like he had it all together even when inside it was all a mess. None of these traits had been passed down to me, unfortunately. I wasn't confident. I wasn't funny. And to make matters worse, I wasn't good-looking. Girls didn't particularly care for me. They'd describe me as a good friend, the sweet guy who could always be counted on to be there when they broke up with the guy who really drove them wild—but certainly I was not boyfriend material.

"This must be uncomfortable for the two of you," said Marie, breaking the awkward silence that descended upon the living room. "I'm just going to say this once. I'm here, if either of you have any questions."

"Why would we have questions about *our* father?" asked Catherine. "I knew him better than anyone else in . . ." She was wound up and itching for a fight, but each time she started to unleash the beast inside, she'd promptly remember how we were trapped at Marie's house. She was already very uncomfortable and didn't want it to get worse. "No, thank you," she added, clearing her senses. "I don't think we have any questions at this time."

"Not all of *us* are so open. There was much damage done when your father left and some of us, even after all these years, are sore about it," said Marie, pausing for a moment. "It sounds funny saying *all of us*, doesn't it? I never thought it'd be this way."

"What do you mean?" asked Catherine.

Marie began stumbling over her words. "Well, it's just that Thomas, I mean your father, didn't really want anything to do with us. He made no secret of that. He ran into some trouble before he left for Wellbourne, bor-

HERE LIES A FATHER

rowed some money that he couldn't pay back, and as for
his family, we were as good as dead to him."

Catherine sat up straight and looked into Marie's face.
"You know, we all have different memories and perspec-
tives of him. He was my father and I want to remember
him in my own way," she said, in the same critical tone
that drove Mom crazy. "He isn't here to defend himself,
is he? I don't want you all bad-mouthing him just because
he's dead. So, if you don't mind, let's end this little walk
down memory lane."

Dad wasn't there to give his side of the story, but I
questioned why Catherine wanted to pretend like his
past didn't exist, like the only important memories were
the ones he'd made with our family. Dad was so private,
to everyone who crossed his path, but especially to me.
Mom had probably known most of his secrets just by
being married to him for so long, and he had slowly been
filling Catherine's ear with tidbits, yet I knew close to
nothing. I craved stories about his life, about when he
was a teenager or when he first met Mom, and I wanted
to hear them whether they were good or bad. Catherine's
outbursts were making it difficult to get either. She was
raising the drawbridge before we even had a chance to
hear anything at all, meaning I'd have to corner some
of these people on my own, which wasn't exactly in my
nature.

I had tried for so long to stay neutral and bite my
tongue, but Catherine was getting on my nerves.

"One second . . ." I cut in. My throat constricted and
it was hard to swallow. I spoke loudly, but in truth I was
terrified and had no idea what I was going to say until it
came out of my mouth. "Catherine, wouldn't you like to

hear about Dad's life before us? I mean, he never told me anything so it might be interesting to hear."

I noticed Marie smirk from one side of her mouth. My sister's eyes opened wide and then closed into two furious slits.

Catherine had a dark side, a way of cutting the legs out from under me. Speaking up had caused catastrophic damage to our united front and she'd make me pay for each and every word. I wouldn't be forgiven until I demonstrated full contrition. I regretted taking a stand against her, but I couldn't see how it wasn't in our best interests to learn more about Dad. Then guilt set in. I remembered nights she made me dinner when Mom worked late, or when she said I could tag along with her and her girlfriends to the movies. When the screaming and threats between Mom and Dad grew too intense to ignore, she'd bring me into her room to play with dolls and listen to cassette tapes. What a selfish asshole I had become. Now I understood why people didn't like me. I should've kept my mouth shut.

"Fine!" she snapped. "That's your choice, but from now on leave me out of it."

The room blurred and the center of my chest seized up. I wanted to punch myself in the face for what I'd said, use the pain to atone for my mistake. I was no better than a spoiled, petulant child.

"That's not fair," I replied, softly.

Marie recognized the painful expression on my face and had pity on me. "Catherine, listen," she said, "I understand he was your father and we aren't here to cast a dark shadow on him. I apologize. Let's change the subject."

Uncle Neil had remained quiet, except for an occasional grunt of agreement or violent cough to loosen the thick phlegm in his throat. His decision to finally open his mouth had more to do with his intentions to leave than to take a side for or against Dad. "Well, ladies and gentleman, I have to hit the road," he said. "Some of us have got to work for a living."

Marie studied her brother. She peered outside and noticed it was dark. "Work? Where? There's no school tomorrow. Whose bus are *you* driving?"

"Christ, Marie. I do a hell of a lot more than just drive the bus."

She stood up and snatched Uncle Neil's empty coffee mug from his hand, shuffling into the kitchen to rinse it out in the sink.

"Got a few maintenance pickups in the morning," he groaned.

"Fine, be gone with you," Marie replied, turning to Catherine and me. "Let me show you two where you'll be sleeping tonight."

"Okay, great," I said, standing up.

Uncle Neil tore out of the house. The door latched behind him and Marie commented snidely about how his drive home would undoubtedly include a detour to the Corner Pocket Lounge, a pool hall in New Brimfield where he played on a league. She used the word *league* loosely, describing it as more of an assembly of tipsy men who drank more highballs than they sank. I was burned out and couldn't wait to be alone with my thoughts. I could tell Catherine was exhausted, but she wouldn't admit it. After yelling at me she had been staring into space. She reacted to Marie's words as if a switch had been flicked and she nodded flatly.

What we all needed was a good night's sleep.

"Thanks for putting us up," I said.

"It's not a problem. Besides, you're *family*," Marie said, trying the word on for size. She explained how she had originally promised Carla the spare bedroom, which held a twin-sized bed, but at the last minute Carla decided to bunk with one of her girlfriends across town.

The mention of her name still irked Catherine, but getting the spare bedroom with the comfortable bed counteracted the poison. I was assigned to Marie's living room couch, the very same blue sectional we had been sitting on, a relic of the mideighties, wrapped around two adjacent walls. Marie set fresh white sheets and an old afghan blanket on the couch for me and told Catherine that the room was already made up for her. Catherine walked away without saying a word.

"Ian, if you get cold tonight just go into the hallway closet and grab yourself an extra blanket," Marie said.

"That's fine, it's fine. I'll be all right."

"The light switch is here. The bathroom is at the end of the hallway if you need it. Everything good?"

"Sure, thanks. You can turn out the light now. I'm pretty tired. I think I'm going to pass right out," I said.

Marie cracked a smile and flicked off the switch. She disappeared down the hallway to her bedroom. I told Marie I was exhausted, but that was a lie. My body was technically fatigued, slow and achy, but my mind was firing like a pinball machine. I couldn't stop ruminating. The man I knew as my father no longer existed. He was dead. His body was ash in the ground. Accepting that I'd never see him again was difficult enough, but now there was a very strong possibility that all my memories of him had been manufactured to avoid a bitter truth.

What made the story about *the others* so improbable was that Dad lived seemingly unaffected by any of it. If it had been true, I could only imagine that the guilt would be crippling. How could any father in his right mind live a normal existence knowing that his children, the ones he barely knew, were just out there in limbo? I closed my eyes and attempted to will myself to sleep, but it was no use. No matter how many times I shifted positions and attempted to ease myself with deep breaths or tranquil thoughts, my restlessness never subsided.

To make matters worse, I didn't want to fall asleep around all these strangers because of my night terrors. They hadn't returned in a long time but could be reignited in stressful situations. Our family doctor told Mom it was fairly common for boys my age with active imaginations and I would grow out of it eventually. He also recommended a prescription—I don't remember what it was called—but Mom refused. The conversation in the examination room had grown rather heated as she rejected the notion of putting her only son on any drug that could alter his mind. She claimed the problem would resolve itself, as the doctor had said, and that she'd rather I not be exposed to foreign substances.

I considered jerking off to calm my senses. The slightest tingling anticipation in my groin meant it would've been so easy to reach down and release all my troubles with a few tugs. I had the perfect visual picked out too, the new girl at school, a redhead named Eveline Ryan. Honestly, she got on my nerves, but she had nice legs, and after what happened I couldn't forget her even if I tried.

* * *

When I first met Eveline she had wandered into Mrs.
Garrett's American literature class after the bell. She was
new to Wellbourne High like me, and the front office had
kept her too long signing paperwork, stroking her delicate sensibilities. We were novelties in a place that rarely
encountered change.

Mrs. Garrett had presented two piles of dog-eared
paperback books to the class. Students slid one book
from the top of the pile and passed the rest back, like
programmed machines on a factory conveyor belt. She
didn't introduce the book until every student received his
or her copy. The book's cover was dark blue with a small
pair of eyes and rosy lips set in the middle, and my copy
had been shoved inside so many backpacks over the years
it no longer stayed closed. On the inside cover someone
had written a giant *15* in black permanent marker for re-
cord-keeping purposes. Lines stamped under *BOOK 15*
held the names of every student who ever had it, one I
recognized from Catherine's graduating class. I scanned
the classroom. Students opened their paperback copies;
some ran their fists down the spines to further bend them
open, and each carefully wrote their names on the empty
lines.

The door opened and a girl with the reddest hair I had
ever seen stepped inside. Everyone was relieved because
it took Mrs. Garrett's attention away from lecturing the
class. The girl closed the door gently behind her, seemingly terrified of slamming it, and marched up to Mrs.
Garrett with her head down like she was in trouble, a
folded piece of paper in her hand and an artsy Bohemian
purse bouncing on her thigh. She whispered something
into Mrs. Garrett's ear.

"Oh yes, Eveline, thank you," she said, checking the class roster attached to a cracked clipboard.

Mrs. Garrett had long curly blond hair with strands of silver, which she kept tied out of her face, an understanding face, and the kind that didn't frighten you when you asked a question. Her classroom was bare except for vintage posters of book jackets from the works of famous authors like Steinbeck, Hemingway, and Whitman. For an English teacher like Mrs. Garrett, an expressive girl such as Eveline Ryan was just the type of student she dreamed about.

"Please have a seat. Everyone, this is Eveline Ryan," said Mrs. Garrett. "Yes, she's late today and this is an example of what not to do, but she's new to town and we'll save the public beheading for another day."

A couple of girls in the back rolled their eyes. They saw her black combat boots, her frayed jean shorts with blue leggings, her long eclectic necklaces, and they didn't understand her—nor did they want to. Eveline got on my last nerve too and she'd been in the room for less than five minutes, yet what I felt toward her wasn't disdain like the girls in the back. I wouldn't have admitted it to anyone, but her presence made me nervous. My heart beat vigorously and my palms got sweaty. I don't know what it was about her, but she got me all worked up.

Eveline searched the classroom for an empty desk without really looking at anybody and the only free spot was next to me. She took off her olive-green coat with fur around the hood. Underneath she wore this white blouse that reminded me of peasants in a Renaissance festival. Her skin looked soft, smooth, and fair in a way that reminded me of cream. She set herself down gently into the plastic seat beside me and slid her small, round behind into the grooved crease. A subtle trail of freckles spread across her cheeks and nose. Fluorescent light from above slipped across the curves of her neck like one of those famous marble sculptures. Her deep red hair, like a tree burning in the night, was draped across one shoulder but kept within a loose braid that allowed thin strands to slide across her face.

Mrs. Garrett droned on about the book she had passed out, how it was a classic story about love lost and yearning to be someone else in life. The truth was, I'd stopped listening. Her voice transformed into this mechanical thrumming and blended with the sound of the ticking radiator. My eyelids drooped heavily downward and the thought of sleep was more desirable than anything I had ever wanted. My neck loosened and my head shifted back and forth; not even an explosion would've roused me. Nothing held my attention for very long, and besides my poor marks in school, my inability to focus may have been the reason why teachers hated me. Teachers loved Catherine, and it was because they expected me to be more like her that they were irritated when I turned out to be such a disappointment.

Someone tapped my arm at just the moment when consciousness surrendered to dream. I jerked upward and my eyes bulged open. *Eveline.* Her fingertips were on my forearm. I looked at her questioningly. Her blue eyes were hypnotic, spellbinding, and reminded me of reflections of the ocean on a sunny day. I twisted forward in my seat. She thought she was helping me, but now I was aggravated about being woken up.

Are you okay? she mouthed at me, flashing an amused grin.

And I just nodded.

Her smooth thighs, pressed against that plastic chair, were all I thought about on Marie's living room couch. In the dark I sat up and glanced out the living room window; a crescent moon partially lit up the forest around the house. I thought again about that morning we met. Never had I expected she'd be more to me than a girl I once sat next to in class. Thinking about her was the safest thing to do. In fact, it's all I could do after she had vanished from school. After what had happened the night of that awful party, I couldn't fault her for leaving town, yet I wished I'd known where she went. Most of all, I hoped that she was okay and not just one more person in my life to whom I never got to say goodbye.

I sat back on Marie's couch and stared up at her off-white ceiling. Another memory came to mind, one I had avoided as long as I could—the day when Catherine called and told me Dad had died.

C HAPTER 5

MOM HAD MADE A LAST-MINUTE DECISION for us to go hiking with a friend named Richard Allen and his daughter Shannon. He was clearly one of her new friends. I'd never heard of him before. She packed a bag with water, sunscreen, granola bars to snack on if we got hungry, and a camera with extra film. Pictures were the most important part for her. She had insisted on not wasting warm weather in New York State. Soon the summer would be upon us, and she needed something significant to take away from it all.

She sang to herself as she straightened up the house and prepared for our day out. I hadn't recalled seeing her so overjoyed in years, which made me happy.

The phone on the dining room wall suddenly rang.

"Could you get that?" she called out from the kitchen.

"Yes, I got it."

"Thanks," she replied in a singsong tone.

I lifted the set off its base. There was an awkward silence as I held it up to my ear. I expected it to be Mr. Allen confirming the time and place of our hiking trip, but it was Catherine.

"Ian?"

"Yes," I said. "What's going on?"

She never called this early in the morning. *Never.*

Something was certainly wrong, no doubt about it. She was pausing too much, weighing her words, and I heard her take a deep breath.

"It's Dad," she said.

"What about him?" I asked, expecting her to say he was in another debacle, like the time he called in the middle of the night because he ran over a horse in our new car. The horse had wandered onto a dark road and he hadn't noticed until it was too late. It broke through the windshield, crushed the front of the car, and shat all over him. Catherine had been devastated and his ordeal became a running punch line.

"He's dead."

"What?"

"I got a call ten minutes ago from Albany Medical Center. They said he passed away in the middle of the night."

Mom hummed busily in the next room.

"He was in the hospital?" I murmured, keeping my voice low so Mom wouldn't hear me. Concealment was my natural reaction.

"Yes, the last two days."

"Why didn't anyone tell me?"

"Mom and I didn't want you to have to worry about it."

"Mom knew?"

"Yes, I told her a few days ago," Catherine said. "And I asked her not to tell you. We didn't think it'd be a long stay."

I didn't respond. Part of my silence was the shock of hearing my father was dead and the other was that I didn't understand why no one had told me. I didn't know what to say. I wasn't good in emotional situations. Actors on television always said, *I'm deeply sorry for your loss*, or, *They're in a better place now*, but how did I really know my dad was in a better place? As far as I knew we lived and died, and then nothing. I wasn't Catholic. Dad and Mom used to be Catholic, but they hated the Church. What if the Church lied about the afterlife? Everyone lied about something.

"How did it happen?" I asked. I expected his death to be extraordinary, like he'd been saving a poor family from a burning house, because nothing with him was ever typical.

"Cancer. The doctors said he was in the advanced stages."

"But . . . I didn't even know that. He never said anything about having cancer. Why didn't he tell us? Why didn't he tell *me*?"

"He had it for years, but ignored the symptoms."

For a moment I felt light-headed, as if I were standing on a high ledge, but it passed quickly and I was in control again. Only one desperate thought crossed my mind: *I can't tell anyone.*

If someone forced the issue I'd have to make up a story. Everyone would find out sooner or later, there was no avoiding that, but at least if I put it off long enough they'd hear it from someone else and save me the trouble. Questions were very dangerous because they opened more doors than they closed. I thought about crying while on the phone with Catherine, because that's what you did when your father died, but I couldn't muster a tear. To be honest, I couldn't remember the last time I had cried. It was cold of me, *as cold as a witch's tit*, like Dad used to say, but it was the truth.

"Listen, I'm flying up to deal with everything," said Catherine.

"Should I tell Mom?"

"She knew about Dad in the hospital, but I'll tell her this later on," she said. "You two aren't going anywhere today, right?"

I glanced at the hiking bag set carefully by the front door. "Nope. Nowhere."

"Good, stay put. I'll call her later. Let me handle it."

As I hung up the phone, Mom glided back into the dining room, light on her feet like an eager dancer making an onstage debut. I looked at her face and noticed she had applied a thin layer of eyeliner with mascara, and her lips were a deeper, glossier red. Her face, usually scrunching in distress, was now loose and uninhibited. She looked like people do after returning from a long vacation. She was truly a beautiful woman. Her long blond hair was up in a ponytail, a style she wore all the time, and she had bright blue eyes like the western sky. She was self-conscious about the larger nose she'd inherited from her side of the family, yet they all had it.

"Who was that?" she asked.

"Oh, nobody."

She studied my face. "Is something wrong? You look upset."

"No, not at all. A telemarketer. I couldn't get off the phone and they kept talking and talking and talking." I just couldn't ruin her day with the truth, not when I saw how excited she was.

"I know, right?" she laughed. "I hate those assholes. Are you ready to go?"

"Let me put on my sneakers."

"And please, Ian, try your best to get along with Mr. Allen and his daughter today. It would really mean a lot to me."

"I will."

"Thanks." She smiled.

On our drive to meet Mr. Allen and Shannon the sun was shining. Thick clouds were scattered across the blue sky. We drove with the windows down and I smelled fresh pollen, mixed with the occasional manure and skunk spray. The sun curved through the car windows like a prism and warmed my chest. It was a beautiful day, but I kept thinking about death. People died every day, even on beautiful days like this. Most people forget that death comes when the sun shines too. They forget the truth about life: it ends.

We pulled into the parking lot next to a squat mountain and pebbles shot out from under our tires. Mom shut off the engine and I saw Mr. Allen and his daughter leaning on the hood of his truck. He wore a yellow fishing shirt with a marlin on the front and old-fashioned Levi's that were too tight. His daughter Shannon had on khaki shorts, a tight black shirt, and low-top Converses. Mom was waving too hard. She spoke first because she always felt obligated to be the social director.

"I'm so glad we all met up today," she said. "This is going to be so much fun."

"I agree, Helen," said Mr. Allen. His daughter Shannon, pouty and disinterested, nodded at me. "Let's set off on a great adventure."

The four of us found the shaded opening to the trail, which twisted in circles around the mountain, ascending slightly until we reached the top. The whole experience was designed for amateurs, not rock climbing but more like leisurely walking up a flight of stairs. After fifteen minutes Mr. Allen was huffing and puffing, stopping to sit on fallen tree trunks or mossy rocks to catch his breath. Mom had enough energy to climb the mountain three times over but kept stopping to make sure he was all right. She kept saying how difficult the climb was to make him feel better.

"Hey Ian," called Mom, "maybe you two should go on ahead while Mr. Allen catches his breath."

"Sure," I said.

"That's a good idea, Helen," said Mr. Allen, panting. "What do you say, Shannon?"

"Thrilled," she answered.

Shannon and I hiked up the trail together and it became harder to see Mom and Mr. Allen behind us. With each step a tree branch or shrub obstructed our view until we couldn't see them at all. And they couldn't see us. We were on our own. A weight was lifted. Each time I looked into Mom's face I thought about Dad being dead and how I was supposed to keep my mouth shut, but it wasn't easy. I was terrified the news of his death would send her into another one of her dark episodes, days spent on the couch watching television with chocolate bars, the drapes pulled tight over the windows so it would be dark in the middle of the day.

Shannon marched in front of me on the trail. I noticed her round ass and liked the way it looked. I watched each side of her tight behind flex and release as she climbed the trail. I imagined what type of underwear she had on. I wasn't a bad guy for staring at her ass, but I felt guilty. I'm a *nice guy*, most of the time, but even good guys look at girls, it's in our nature. That didn't make me bad. It didn't even make me bad for not telling Mom about Dad's death. I was protecting her. Catherine was better with Mom's feelings than I was, anyway. I wouldn't know where to begin. I couldn't even cry and I got uncomfortable around emotional people.

Shannon jerked to the side and made eye contact with me. "Can you believe those two?" She stopped and waited for me to catch up.

"What do you mean?"

"They drag us to this boring mountain and they make us go ahead of them because they can't handle it. Well, I mean, my father can't handle it. What a lard-ass. I tell him he needs to eat better and exercise but he doesn't listen to me. Parents never do."

I was unsure how to respond. "That's messed up," I said, regretting the words as soon as they left my mouth.

She stepped out onto an enormous flat rock that extended from the trail like an observation deck, and from it we could see the entire valley below, roads like dark veins spreading across the ground, cornfields laid in perfect rectangles that vanished into the horizon. How did they even get those rows so straight? Shannon waited for me to step onto the rock beside her. She was breathing heavily now and a layer of sweat below her hairline glistened in the sun.

"They're probably going to talk about us. If we're getting along, that kind of crap," she said.

I laughed nervously.

"I think my dad likes your mom."

"Really?"

"Oh yeah, they're probably hooking up right now, especially since we're out of the picture." She laughed.

"I don't know, maybe," I answered. *Why am I being so awkward?*

"My mother died when I was five," she said. "It's been me and Dad ever since. Where's your father?"

I scoured my mind for the right story. "He works in Albany."

"Oh, so you're parents aren't divorced?"

"Nope, not that I know of."

Shannon furrowed her brow. I picked up a few rocks and started tossing them over the side of the mountain to see what would happen.

"Well, kissing or not, they seem to get along."

"Yup."

"They could do it, you know. Nobody's around," she said, looking from side to side. "And anybody could. I've done a lot more than kissing." She peered at me intensely for a moment. "I saw you staring at me before."

"What? I . . . uh . . . what are you talking about?"

"Down the hill. You did. It's okay. I have a nice ass." She turned in place and looked at her backside.

I didn't say a word. I scanned the valley, pretending that she hadn't said what she said. Pretending it wasn't happening. That worked sometimes.

"So, I take it you're shy?" she said, running her fingertips along my forearm.

"I don't know." I no longer felt in control of myself and I looked at her like a scolded dog does his master.

She smiled. "You're not the one to make a move either, huh?"

My face began to tingle.

Her hands hovered above her khaki shorts and her fingers gently unfastened the button. Her zipper made a metallic noise as she pulled it apart. Underneath she wore a pair of light-pink panties. "I let my boyfriends touch, but that's as far as I go." She cocked her head to one side and her lustful eyes were dilated.

"Are you serious?" I whispered, even though nobody was around, and I shook slightly, as if a cold wind had swept up the face of the mountain. My crotch was throbbing and I felt myself swell against the side of my pants.

She was crazy. Girls didn't talk like that. She'd said her mother died when she was young, so maybe being raised by a father made her more like a guy. But I was a guy and I never talked like that. I wanted so badly to let my fingers explore her, but how could I do that to Mom? I promised Mom I'd be on my best behavior so I wouldn't ruin her day with Mr. Allen. Catching us fooling around on the mountaintop would certainly wreck the day.

"Well, if you aren't interested, then . . ." She began pulling up the zipper on her shorts.

The next thing I knew my lips were on hers. We panted like dogs in heat, the skin around our mouths wet, goose-pimpled, hands groping each other's backs, my hands squeezing her ass, and that's when I slid my hand under her shirt and took hold of one of her large breasts. Her bra was smooth silk and I squeezed, massaged in circular motions. It was the first time I had my hand under a girl's shirt. She moaned lightly. I had never been so excited in my entire life—until we heard voices.

"Shannon? Ian? Are you two up there?"

Shit. I took my hand from her breast and released my mouth from hers like a suction cup. She fixed her own shirt and tied her hair back. I took a couple of deep breaths and adjusted the crotch of my pants.

"Yes, over here," I said. My voice cracked.

Shannon sat down on the rock slab facing away from me and she appeared to be laughing to herself. I stood in silence with my hands in my pockets, staring at her back and waiting for Mom and Mr. Allen to catch up. They turned the corner. I don't think they saw us, but maybe they did. They could have been covering up to avoid an uncomfortable situation. I did that sometimes.

"Hey, you two," said Mr. Allen.

"Hey, Daddy," Shannon said sweetly, standing up and draping one arm over his shoulder.

"How's the climb going?"

"Fine." She spoke in this nauseating baby voice.

He put his arm around her and hugged her close. "Oh, my little girl."

"Are you still tired, Daddy?"

"No, but thanks for asking. Helen and I found this fantastic inscription in a rock over there. Someone chiseled their name and the year 1892. Come see."

Mr. Allen took Shannon down the trail to display his great discovery and Mom stepped onto the rock slab next to me.

"So, what do you think?" she asked.

"About?"

"Mr. Allen and Shannon."

"He's all right, but she seems a little out there. They're fine."

What could I have said about a man wanting to spend so much time with my mother when my father was dead? All the blood had rushed back up to my brain finally and

I began thinking clearly. I remembered Catherine's phone call. And I remembered Dad. Life was so random.

"Just *fine*?" said Mom. She was disappointed. "You know, you always do this. You act so strange and melodramatic sometimes. I'm a little frustrated here because it doesn't seem like you're making an effort."

"That's not true."

"Yes it is, and I would appreciate it if you stopped being so selfish and put on a goddamn smile for five minutes. It's like you don't even want to be here."

I flashed my teeth in a demonic grin. "Well, I'm sorry. My mind is on other things."

"Like what? Yourself? That makes sense. You've been acting so selfish lately, I can't believe how selfish you've been."

"You don't want to know what's on my mind."

"Tell me."

I stood in silence.

"For Christ's sake, tell me!"

"Fine! I wasn't supposed to say anything but Catherine called this morning and Dad is dead."

For a moment we both stood speechless. The only sound was the distant crunching of leaves and branches from Mr. Allen and Shannon in the brush.

"What?"

"Dad died. He had cancer but none of us knew."

She looked out across the valley. I expected to see tears rolling down her cheeks, her fists pounding, bitter screams of lament, an emotional fallout, but instead she turned to me, annoyed. "Your father really knows how to ruin everything."

SATURDAY

C HAPTER 6

THE NEXT MORNING I AWAKENED on Marie's couch earlier than usual. I didn't sleep well because an intense beam of sunlight from the living room window landed directly on my face. I thought about what Mom always said about staying in hotels. They were nice because she got a break from being responsible for everything, yet the unfamiliar surroundings made it impossible to actually get a good night's sleep. Rarely was she able to stay in a hotel—we didn't have that kind of money to throw around. What I thought about next was how difficult it must've been for her over the years, essentially being the only person overseeing our lives while Dad was away at one of his mysterious jobs that never seemed to last very long.

The air in Marie's living room was dry and my throat was sore. I overheard activity in the kitchen and realized it was impossible to go back to dozing. When I finally sat up I noticed Catherine, already showered and redressed in her clothes from yesterday. She was tightening the lid of a coffee thermos she'd borrowed from Marie's cabinet.

"Good morning," she said, vigorously sorting through her purse.

"Hey," I replied, still foggy. "What's going on?"

"I called that tire shop a few minutes ago and they're towing our car now. Thought I'd get down there and make sure they don't dawdle," she said, finally setting her purse down on the kitchen table next to the thermos, once its contents were arranged just so. "We've got a long drive today and I'd like to start as soon as possible."

I looked around the room from my vantage point on the couch. "Is Marie up?"

"Not yet."

I yawned and scratched the back of my skull. I had no bags to pack and a shower without a change of clothes was pointless in my opinion. The only thing I had to do was put on my shoes and I'd be ready to leave; yet it didn't feel right. I didn't want to leave without saying goodbye to Marie, thanking her for her hospitality and exchanging phone numbers or e-mail addresses to keep in touch. She was family, after all. And not to belabor the point—I knew Catherine was well aware of it—but Marie had gone through the trouble of inviting other relatives to meet us later that day and memorialize Dad in a sort of reverse wake. I didn't intend to take sides against Catherine a second time, but it didn't seem right to scamper off. Rather than make a scene, I silently protested by taking my time getting up, hoping Marie would make an early appearance.

"Are you ready?" asked Catherine. "Do you need to use the bathroom or anything?"

"No, I don't think so."

"Good. Let's get a move on then."

At some point Catherine had also contacted a local cab company and requested a driver to pick us up at Marie's. I tied my shoes and drank about half a cup of coffee before we heard a terse beep in the driveway and spotted a beat-up cab waiting outside, its bright yellow presence hovering anxiously. Marie still hadn't surfaced and as Catherine dragged me out the front door, I felt heaviness in the base of my stomach. Catherine, on the other hand, breathed a sigh of relief once we'd both climbed into the backseat and slammed the doors shut. The driver took us to Chuck's Tires, which wasn't as far as I had expected. If we had wanted to save money and had given ourselves a twenty-minute head start, we probably could've walked.

The morning air was cool and clear. A loose mist spread across New Brimfield, remnants of the previous day's storm which the sun had begun to dry out. I looked across downtown. A handful of redbrick buildings, shops, and cafés with low-rent apartments on the second floor formed a square at the center of town. A tower in the middle held a clock that appeared as if it hadn't run in years.

I wondered if Marie had awakened and made the realization that she was alone in the house, that her guests had ditched her. Being alone wasn't so bad, yet I still felt guilty about it.

I began thinking about Dad and how he'd been living alone in that Albany apartment before he died.

After Florida he didn't come straight home to us. He relocated to Albany instead, about a thirty-minute drive, because that's where the real opportunities were. Mom and I visited him once. His apartment was not what I had expected. I knew it would be a small place, based on his description. A studio is what he called it. The truth was, he probably snatched up whatever room was cheapest. He had stayed in worse places over the years.

The hallway leading to his room was beige and I was afraid of slipping on the freshly waxed floor. Fluorescent lights flickered above. Brown doors lined both sides with room numbers labeled in gold letters. I smelled what could only be described as a combination of bleach and vegetable soup. In one room, the television volume was up so high that we heard a game show and a cheering audience through the wall. I wondered how long Dad was planning on staying. We would never be a real family again until he came home.

We finally located his room and Mom knocked. The spy hole went dark as someone behind it scrutinized us.

"Who is it?" said a menacing voice.

"Who the hell do you think?" Mom shot back.

"One second."

I heard the clicking of dead bolts and the sliding of a chain.

Dad stood in the open doorway; his gray hair was longer than usual and in disarray, like he had just woken up. He resembled a bloated version of Charles Bronson, from the *Death Wish* movies, not the younger, tanner Bronson in the old Westerns. His hair, yellowing at the tips from nicotine, was parted to one side and brushed across his forehead. He'd styled it that way for as long as I could remember. A gray, bushy mustache covered his top lip. He had grown it long before I was born and I'd never seen him without it. What stood out to me was how surprisingly well dressed he was, in a pullover sweater with khakis and brown loafers, yet his clothes hung loose because he was skinnier than before. At the time I thought nothing of it. Dad was never a large man.

"Well, it's been a long time, sport," he said, patting my shoulder.

I wasn't angry over not having seen him for months, but his hand hovered over my shoulder for longer than necessary. I very subtly stepped to the side, as though shifting my weight to another leg, and his hand slipped off.

"Yes, it has," I said.

"Well come in, come in to my humble abode."

Mom and Dad didn't kiss at the door. They probably didn't want to make me uncomfortable or embarrassed. Teenagers hated seeing their parents show affection. Dad closed the door behind us and peeked out of the spy hole one last time to make sure no one else was there. He relocked the dead bolts and reattached the chain. A narrow hallway with high ceilings opened up to a large room: a bedroom, dining room, compact kitchen, and living room in one.

His apartment walls were white and the floor was covered with a green industrial-grade carpet, the kind installed in offices or elementary schools. A small round table with three mismatched wooden chairs were arranged next to the entrance to the kitchen and Mom took a seat. I followed her lead and sat across from her. Dad stood in place with his hands on his waist.

"Did you find the place all right?"

"We did." Mom slid a cigarette out of her shiny new pack and casually lit it with a book of matches from Dad's kitchen table, taking a long drag, eyeing the apartment. "You picked one hell of a place here," she said. She exhaled smoke from her nose like a charging bull.

Dad nervously thought of an explanation as she

picked a loose piece of tobacco from her lip. "Well, it's a last-minute thing, only temporary," he said, turning to me, beaming. "You should see some of the nuts in this place, Ian. Certifiable, all of them! This asshole George, he lives next door, still owes me thirty dollars from a poker game last week, but the best part is that this son of a bitch got hit in the head years ago and shits himself if he's left alone too long. Then there's this *woman* across the hall, she used to turn tricks for—"

"Is this why you asked us here?" interrupted Mom. "To gossip about complete strangers?"

"Well, no. I wanted to see my wife and son. Can't a man do that?"

Mom sighed, took another hit from her cigarette. The tip flashed bright orange.

I studied his apartment. A creepy painting of an opera clown hung on the wall. A little girl in a white-and-pink-collared dress with matching bobby socks sat on his lap. She was crying and the clown gently wiped her tears away with his finger. I hated clowns. I've hated them ever since my cousins convinced me to watch a horror movie where an evil clown ate children in the sewer. Dad noticed me studying the painting, and even though I had a disgusted look on my face, he was compelled to explain how it reminded him of Catherine. He grew misty-eyed and it made me angry. I didn't want my father to be a blubbering fool, especially after not seeing him for months.

The three of us sat awkwardly around the circular kitchen table, not sure of what to say next, pretending to be a considerate family.

"So, where have you two been staying all this time?" asked Dad.

"You already know the answer to that," said Mom.

"Oh, yes. I must've forgot." He paused. "Helen, what have you been doing for work?"

"I told you that too."

"Well, holy shit, don't jump down my goddamn throat!" he shouted. "Is it a crime for a husband to ask his wife a question?"

"No, but how many times do I have to repeat it?" said Mom pointedly. "I know what you really want to ask me and the answer is no. Nothing has happened!"

"Well," said Dad, carefully collecting his thoughts, "how do I know that? You two have been there for weeks without me, who's to say there hasn't been—"

"For Christ's sake, not in front of your son!" snapped Mom, widening her eyes.

Dad turned and looked at me. He had forgotten I was even in the room. "Ian, sport, could you do me a favor and get something from the closet by the front door? I have these pamphlets from my new job and I want to show you."

"Where's the new job?"

"It's called the Whittaker, a real fancy place, five stars, cloth napkins, crumbing tools, sparkling water, all of that shit," he said, grinning. "Morons ordering ten-dollar beers and fifteen-dollar martinis. I stole some of their pamphlets for you. Go find them, will you?"

If what Dad said about the Whittaker was true, it meant we'd all be able to live together again. I leaped up from the kitchen table and entered Dad's closet on a mission to find those pamphlets. Empty cardboard boxes were scattered on cheap wire shelving. I tried to guess what might've come in them, but his apartment was bare.

I peeked inside a few, discovering only cobwebs and mold spores.

Against the back wall of the closet—on the bottom shelf as if intentionally hidden—I found Dad's old jewelry box. I remembered how it used to sit on his bedroom dresser, made of wood with a lid of smooth blue marble. The lid was a sculpted relief of a schooner, as white as ivory, sailing across blue skies dabbled with thin clouds. On afternoons when I was alone, I riffled through Dad's keepsakes. I'd go through his rings, tie clips, and cuff links, and even hold his father's gold pocket watch in the palm of my hand. I'd wind it up a few turns to watch time pass me by, gripping the cold metal.

Mom said the pocket watch had been in the Daly family for generations. My grandfather died when Dad was fifteen, a massive heart attack, I had heard, but by a stroke of luck he was able to pass it on to my father beforehand. Dad never verified the story or even mentioned the watch to me. It wasn't any of my business, but Mom insisted he intended to give it to me someday, a special gift for when I was old enough.

I carefully lifted the old jewelry box from the shelf. Thick dust covered the lid, which nearly fell off because a hinge screw was missing. I pushed it up with my index finger, expecting it to be full, like when I was a boy, but only a few broken trinkets remained. There was a ripped dollar bill, broken pieces of chintzy metal, car wash coins, and wooden beer tokens. I laid the box back on the shelf and walked out of the closet, hearing Mom and Dad from the kitchen.

The tone of their conversation reminded me of those nights when their aggravated voices reverberated down the shadowy hallway past my bedroom. They rarely kept quiet with anything they did and my door was always slightly ajar at night. There was something comforting about hearing their squabbles because at least they weren't ignoring each other and they were both home.

Their words grew clearer as I approached.

"You keep saying that, like a goddamn parrot. Nothing . . . nothing. Well, it's been months and what about before that? And what the fuck am I supposed to do? You can't blame a man for being a man."

"What do you want to hear?"

"Tell me about the next time I'm getting mine!"

"Your what?"

"If nothing is happening, like you say, then when do I get mine?" he pressed.

"You son of a bitch," she replied.

I slid my back down the surface of the hallway wall and listened for a moment. Sometimes, when I was a boy, I found out what was *really* going on this way, but most of the time I only overheard information that I couldn't reconcile. Mom suddenly hushed Dad and spoke just above a whisper.

"Lower your voice," she demanded. "We came here to visit, so Ian could see his father, not for me to take any more of your shit."

"Oh, here it comes again, the fucking martyr, wah, wah, wah . . ."

I cleared my throat loudly and tapped my feet, announcing my presence, before stepping out from behind the corner. I needed to interrupt, before things got too heated. I rejoined them at the table and cut through whatever tension had built up. Once again, I was a force for peace.

"I didn't find any pamphlets," I said.

Everything fell silent for a moment except for an airplane flying over the building on its way to the Albany airport. The walls gently thrummed and we all gathered our thoughts.

"Oh really? I could've sworn I had some back there," said Dad. "Fuck it. The point is I'm working and it's good for all of us."

"Is that really the point?" said Mom.

Dad glared at her with his eyes bulging, jaw clenched, and the faintest blue vein pulsing across his reddish forehead. Mom grinned and then gracefully slipped a new cigarette from her pack on the table. I heard the sizzle of the flame on the dried tobacco. She peered down into her purse and dug around for something.

Dad stood up and walked to the other side of the apartment, breathing heavily, and pushed aside cheap floral curtains hanging above a window. "Ian, come here and look at this." He positioned himself at the window and I joined him. "Isn't it great?" he said. "Look."

There was still enough radiant light outside to see miniature cars and people below, like ants carrying on uneventful lives, unaware they were being watched by the two of us.

"What are we looking for exactly?" I asked. "The parking lot?"

"No, not that, you smart-ass. *That*." He pointed to a deteriorating sailboat on a trailer seven floors below.

"A boat?"

"Not just any boat. It's *my* boat! We never got a

chance to sail in Florida, but better late than never. What do you think?"

"We don't know how to sail," I said. "What are you going to do with it?"

"What the hell do you think I'm going to do with it? I'm going to sail it." Dad explained how he bought it off a lowlife on the third floor, to sail down the Hudson River and merge into the Atlantic Ocean, somewhere near New York City, and head down the eastern seaboard. The sea was tumultuous, he said, but so was life, and as long as he stayed parallel to the coast he'd be close enough to get rescued if anything serious happened.

The problem was the boat was in horrible shape, that much was clear from seven stories up, and Dad didn't even know how to swim.

C HAPTER 7

CATHERINE AND I SAT IN THE LOBBY of Chuck's Tires on yellow plastic chairs for almost an hour before the man with a button-down uniform, navy-blue with patches, hovered over us with a clipboard holding the invoice for the work done. Catherine had been staring into space, contemplating something, and I had been looking at the pictures of some European car magazines fanned out across an end table.

"Think we're all set, Ms. Daly," he said.

We both stood up and followed him to the front counter. He circled around and slid the clipboard across, reaching out for a set of hooks that held our keys.

"Can't tell what caused that flat, but it sure as hell ripped the whole tire apart," he said. "For a new tire and labor, it'll only come to $136.78. The tow is on us."

Catherine rolled her eyes in frustration. She dug in her purse for the cash and I knew it was more than she had expected to spend that weekend, especially as a college student with no steady income.

"I just need you to initial here and here, and sign at the bottom," he said, then tossed the keys to Catherine.

She snatched up the yellow carbon copy of the paperwork. We located the orange hatchback on the side of the building. Catherine planned our trajectory home using the same worn-out directions we had printed days earlier, the same set that had caused us so much trouble in the first place. I remembered thinking, over the course of our drive to New Brimfield on Friday, that not a thing in the world was as bad as feeling lost. *Off track. Powerless.* And then suddenly realizing there was absolutely nothing you could do about it. Catherine and I had had the foresight to print out our directions ahead of time, but we failed to anticipate that certain country roads weren't clearly marked.

During that drive on Friday we had both squinted quietly through thick raindrops that crawled across the windshield like spiders, our wipers leaving thin streaks behind. I watched them slide from one end of the window to the other, producing a grinding sound similar to that of squeezing an inflated balloon. Negotiating the desolate network of back roads had proved daunting. Irritation took hold and we replied curtly to each other's questions. Catherine clearing her throat or loudly sniffing up each nostril was *all* I heard. I squeezed my hands into tight fists to relieve my agitation.

We passed the same caved-in red barn three times in a row. Soon I began to feel that Catherine somehow blamed me. She never said as much, but I was familiar with how we operated in the Daly family. Let someone else make the decisions and be the first to strike when things didn't work out. Like whenever Mom entrusted Dad to pay the rent and utilities on time. I could've told her he'd forget by the end of the month, but as soon as the past-due notices started arriving she'd be outraged, as if it were all a big surprise, calling him a *useless fuck-up* and *good for nothing*.

"According to this we are only twenty-five miles away," Catherine said.

"Let's not get ahead of ourselves yet, I haven't seen any signs for New Brimfield." Not that I had meant to be pessimistic, but it was just easier to brace for any possible disappointments by not growing too hopeful.

"Look for yourself," Catherine demanded, tossing the directions into my lap. "One inch equals fifty miles and the distance now is about half an inch."

I rolled my eyes. "We'll see."

"We *are* on the right path now," Catherine said. "I can feel it." A slight grin had appeared at the edges of her mouth. I liked her much better that way, in a good mood, which appeared to be her overall disposition after she had permanently left home for college.

"Too bad you didn't *feel it* earlier," I said.

"What is that supposed to mean? You had the same map as me and I didn't see you making any headway."

Her optimism faded like a flashlight with dead batteries and rather than belabor the point, I decided my work was done.

"This is the road," she said to no one in particular.

Minutes later we had spotted a blue road sign proclaiming, *Welcome to New Brimfield*, and Catherine only gloated for a few minutes before droning on about what should and shouldn't be said when we arrived at the cemetery, drawing up the ground rules. She had undoubtedly drawn up a verbal list with Mom in advance to avoid discussing certain sensitive details about *our* family. That level of strategizing reminded me of a lawyer preparing a

witness for cross-examination and it was too exhausting
to keep straight.

"Now remember, we're going to be in and out, have
Dad buried and then get home before things get weird."

"Okay," I said.

She lifted her foam cup for a triumphant sip of overly
sweetened coffee, when the car had hit a rather large and
unavoidable pothole. The cold coffee shot out of the lid
like a geyser and a pool of creamy liquid landed on our
map.

I lifted the printed directions. A puddle of coffee slid
down one side and landed on the floorboard.

"Just the map," I said, wiping it down with a brown
napkin I had stuffed in the door panel. The damage was
done. Some of the liquid had instantly settled on the paper, leaving behind a giant caramel stain. "Not a big deal."

She snatched the directions from my hands and began
anxiously fanning the paper out, hoping to salvage our
only piece of reliable information. Once she was satisfied
that nothing else could be done to mitigate the damage,
she folded the stained papers and carefully slid them into
the driver's-side door panel. They'd be safer with her. The
steady beat of the rain and the mechanized snapping of
the wipers set me into a sort of hypnotic state. In minutes
we'd arrive at the gates of the New Brimfield Memorial
Cemetery and meet Dad's brother for the first time. The
burial would follow and after that I didn't quite know
what to expect. I thought about all the changes we had
already gone through in the past two years. How Dad
was now dead and how I had barely considered that fact
at all.

* * *

I stood in an empty parking space at Chuck's Tires. Catherine continued studying the directions, the engine thrumming, waiting for me to climb in the car so we could finally leave New Brimfield. Our new shiny tire stood out in stark contrast to all the wear that had accumulated on the other three. I observed the early-morning bustle of New Brimfield's village center, people carrying on with their seemingly important lives, and I thought about my next move.

Catherine rolled down the passenger-side window. "Are you getting in so we can go home? I swear you're so scatterbrained sometimes."

Going home.

Home? What was home? We always had places to live, or somewhere to hang our hats, as Mom used to say, but actually comprehending *home* in my head was like grasping at vapor. It was always dependent on a series of conditions. *One day, if your father gets that job. One day, if we get the car back. One day, if I have the time off. One day, if we have the money. One day.* All we had to do was wait for it—that *one day*—yet it always managed to slip through our fingers. I grew pensive in that parking space. Why should I keep putting off that which I could do today?

I shifted my gaze from the village center back to the car. "Actually . . . no . . . I don't think I'm going."

Catherine laughed as if I were pulling a prank. She leaned over and pushed open the car door. "Seriously, though, we're wasting time here. We've got to get going. Get in."

"I'm staying."

Catherine sighed, shut off the engine, and got out as

well. She circled the back of the car to face me. "To do what, exactly?"

"Marie went through all this trouble to invite the family today. This might be our only chance to meet them. Aren't you the least bit interested?"

"No," she barked. "Trust me, you don't want to hear what they've got to say. Besides, Mom is expecting us home. I have a flight to catch and Mom has plans for you two."

"Plans?"

"Remember Robert, our cousin?"

"I think so."

"He's getting married and Mom wants you to go with her to the ceremony."

As usual, Mom's timing was impeccable. She had likely accepted the invitation to my cousin Robert's wedding months earlier, but had failed to mention it to me. And in a cowardly fashion, she'd tasked Catherine with delivering the news. It didn't matter that my father had died. She'd attend the wedding as if nothing had happened. I tried to imagine how she would react if I told her I wasn't going. She'd take it as a personal affront, of course, that I was intentionally derailing her efforts to lead a happy life. Even with the plausible excuse of burying my father, a refusal would set her into a righteous rage. *I had to go.* At least so I didn't upset her at such a difficult time in her life. I had to be there for her because no one else really was.

"When?"

"Sunday night," Catherine sneered. "You better go."

"Fine, yes, I can go. I can do both. I'll stay here un-til Sunday morning and then . . ." I desperately searched

Main Street for a solution to my problem and spotted a small green *BUS* sign hanging from an awning. "I'll take a bus home on Sunday afternoon."

"Whatever," she said, rolling her eyes. "If you're late and miss it, you can deal with Mom's wrath."

"That's fine with me."

Catherine shook her head and got back in the car. Before pulling out, she rolled up the driver's-side window and flashed me this look I'll never forget, like a prison guard watching a death row inmate being led to his own demise. No matter what happened over the rest of the weekend, I was a dead man in her eyes, and I'd have to deal with the consequences. If I'd been smart like her I would've climbed back in the car and driven back to Wellbourne, played the dutiful son for Mom at cousin Robert's wedding, and forgotten that I'd ever met the Daly clan. The truth was, I hadn't been playing it very smart lately.

I waved goodbye as the car shrank in the distance. For the first time I was alone. Not just me standing alone in a narrow parking lot, but rather free of the influence of Mom, Catherine, or any of my ridiculous friends whom I no longer wanted anything to do with. I stepped onto the sidewalk that led me back toward Marie's house. I'd be at her front door in minutes.

Hopefully she'd be awake so I could calmly explain what had happened between Catherine and me.

CHAPTER 8

I LOOSELY KNEW THE WAY BACK to Marie's house from having stared out the cab window as we drove into town. Cars passed me from both directions, and with each step I attempted to piece together my explanation for Marie. The sidewalk I took ran parallel to Main Street and was cracked, as if someone had taken a sledgehammer to it. Huge meandering roots and harsh winters had bored through the concrete like it were soapstone. Looking at the cracks reminded me of the second time I ran into Eveline Ryan, a few weeks after school started but before that nerve-racking night I'd never forget.

I had stepped off the school bus at the end of the day, believing myself to be alone, when Eveline called out behind me. She shouted my name. I pretended I hadn't heard her, but she eventually caught up with me. She wore green khaki shorts, tight and low on her hips, with dark leggings and a ratty black T-shirt advertising some punk band I'd never heard of. That pretentious Bohemian bag was still slung over her shoulder. I shook her hand firmly, a gesture she probably wasn't used to receiving from high school boys. She played dumb and asked if I was the guy who sat next to her in Mrs. Garrett's class and I nodded. Then she demanded that we walk home from the bus stop together.

Giant bare oak trees hung over the street and I can still visualize the two of us carefully stepping over the cracks in the sidewalk, as if physical contact was prohibited. A few inches of snow blanketed the ground, left over from a storm earlier that week. The sidewalk was narrow so I let her occupy most of it. I half stepped in the snow. After spending two years in Florida I had a hard time adjusting to the winters again. They had never been my favorite season, and once back in Wellbourne I had to wear extra layers to stop my teeth from chattering at the bus stop.

"I love the winter," she said. "Especially during the first snowfall."

"What's the big deal about snow?" I asked.

"My entire family goes on a skiing trip every winter, it's the one thing I look forward to all year," she said, picking up a handful of snow, rolling it into a ball, and throwing it across the street. Then she shrugged. "But since I moved here it's been harder for us all to get together."

"I came back from Florida in January, but I was born here in Wellbourne," I said. "I didn't miss the snow."

"What about your family?"

"What about them?"

"You didn't move back all by yourself, right?" She laughed.

"Well, that's what I meant: my family, we moved back," I said, chuckling nervously. She made me uneasy.

"What do they do?"

"My father is a hotel manager at one of those huge vacation resorts," I said, quietly offended at her line of questioning. "That's why he's still down in Florida right now. He had to train his replacement before leaving."

This was half true. Dad had managed a hotel when I was younger, but a small one in Wellbourne. She wouldn't know the difference anyway.

"Was it at Disney?" she asked. "I love Disney."

"Um, no, nothing like that," I said, noticing how much my answer seemed to disappoint her. "It was one of Disney's competitors, though, real big, with resorts all over the world, but you probably haven't heard of it."

"Really, what's it called?"

Questions. Why so many questions? "It's called . . ." I said, searching for inspiration. "It's called the Willowy Oaks."

"Hmm, I haven't heard of that."

"I told you."

"And what about your mom?"

"My mom? She's in the restaurant business."

"Oh really, what does she do?"

"A little bit of everything. She's out of town right now. Consulting."

"So are you living alone right now?"

"Um, sort of, yes, I am."

Half straddling the sidewalk was harder than I expected. I lost my balance more than once. Periodically, I was forced to hop while struggling to keep the space between us. I looked at her and imagined that a lot of guys probably wanted her. Not that I cared. Other guys probably made her feel nervous or uncomfortable with their directness, but I didn't want to be the other guys, so I kept the conversation dull and shallow. I could've been more interesting to her if I wanted, but my aim wasn't to get into her pants with a bunch of fake, silly questions about her life.

To be honest, her life seemed obnoxious to me. Visualizing it posed no surprises. Her parents likely worked secure nine-to-five jobs. Daddy probably had a boat docked on the Hudson River, matched the family in white yachting outfits over the holidays, sipped mimosas for brunch, and avoided runaway skiffs in the harbor with Uncle Ronnie the millionaire venture capitalist. Mommy probably served on the PTA, taught the girls ballet at the community center, and volunteered two weeks a year packing canned food at a Guatemalan mission. She probably worked part-time, just to stay "busy." *But let's face it: they don't need the money.* I didn't know if any of that was true, but it certainly painted an irritating picture.

One thing I kept watching was Eveline's stride. She was impressively graceful as if her movements were rehearsed in a studio ahead of time. I could tell she was the type of girl who was rarely caught off guard; she had this quiet confidence about her. It could be the end of the world and she'd stroll past without any concern at all, smiling at the falling snow.

"Are you bored around here?" she asked me.

"I don't know, are you?"

"No, I don't go out much, but I'm not bored. When I'm not at school I spend most of my time practicing."

"Practicing what?" I asked.

"The piano. My mom signed me up for lessons when I was six and I've been playing ever since."

"That sounds nice."

"Maybe you could come over and hear me play sometime?" She grinned.

"Sure."

There was a particularly long lull in the conversation and then she turned to me. "What did you say?"

"I didn't say anything."

"You seem like you wanted to say something?"

"Nope."

"Oh, come on. What were you going to say?" she asked playfully.

I avoided eye contact with her and glanced up into the cloudy sky.

"I have an idea," she said with a devious grin.

"What's that?"

"I'm starving and my parents are working late. I'd love a slice of pizza. What do you say?"

Mom was also working late and pizza sounded fantastic. We turned around and walked together to the only pizzeria in town, the Leaning Tower of Pizza. I understood the play on words, and it was sort of funny, but the giant, crooked tower next to the sign above the restaurant was a little much. The inside of the restaurant was covered with maps of Italy, autographs from famous Italian actors like Sylvester Stallone, and framed paintings of the Colosseum and other ancient ruins. A small crew of young Italian guys manned the counter. Each wore sweaty white undershirts and aprons covered with flour. An older man with gray hair on the sides of his head shoveled pies in the oven like a coal stoker in the bowels of a steamship.

I ordered for us both and they were quick. In minutes, they handed us steaming slices. I ordered a Pepsi for myself and a peach ice tea for her because she didn't drink soda. I seasoned my slice with Parmesan cheese, garlic, salt and pepper, and presented each container to

Eveline first, for her approval, before shaking some onto her slice as well. I paid too. I didn't want to seem like the kind of asshole who didn't buy a girl a slice. We took our pizza and walked to an empty red booth in the corner. She turned and waved at a guy behind the counter who I recognized as the fighter from my first night at the Wellbourne Boxing Club.

"Do you know him?" I asked.

"Who, Enzo? Yeah. He's a really nice guy," she said. "His family owns this place. You know him?" Based on the tone of her voice, there was something seriously wrong with me for not having known Enzo.

"I met him at the Wellbourne Boxing Club a few weeks ago."

"You box?"

I laughed before she could. "Well, I wouldn't say that. I mean, I've been to the gym, learning, but I wouldn't say I box."

"Yeah, but you're doing it, right? So why wouldn't that mean you box?"

"I guess it does." I didn't know what to say next. I looked at Enzo behind the counter. I understood why girls made it a point to meet him. He had olive skin, tightly barbered hair like black silk, and he was buff too, probably from years of boxing. Girls probably came to the restaurant to watch him work, and got all hot and woozy whenever he walked past their table, having to fan themselves with empty paper plates.

"Enzo was one of the first guys I met in Wellbourne."

"Really?" I said. "Did you two date at all?"

"No," she giggled. "That's silly. Guys and girls can be friends, you know."

No they can't, I thought.

"Why . . . are you jealous?" she asked.

"Ha! No, why would I be? I just know he's a good-looking guy and a lot of girls would be interested in dating him. That's all."

"You think he's good-looking?" she asked, grinning.

"Yeah, don't you? I mean, not like I want to date the guy," I said, panicking a bit, and then I let go and laughed again.

"There's a smile." She gently shifted in her seat, bringing one of her legs on top of the other, and tied back her curly red hair. She dropped a white straw in her peach ice tea, her skin sticky from the heat of the pizza ovens which kept the inside of the shop rather humid, and she took a long sip from the bottle. We sat quietly for a moment and she looked me in the eye, smiled, and blew softly on her slice of pizza to cool it. She bit off the cheesy tip and dabbed her mouth with a napkin.

"How is it?" I asked.

"Mmm, hmm, good," she said, chewing and putting her thumb up.

I watched her eat. She hadn't looked over at Enzo once since we last mentioned him. I didn't know if that necessarily meant anything, because girls were real experts at hiding their true feelings. I couldn't fathom how they kept everything so bottled up. Their minds could be swirling in all directions, suffering from burning desire or rage, yet no one had the slightest idea. Eveline could be criticizing my every word and laughing to herself about how pathetic I acted. I wasn't sure if I could trust girls.

We finished our slices and carried the empty paper plates to a plastic garbage can next to the door. Eveline

only drank half of her peach ice tea so she secured the cap
and slipped it in her bag. As we left, she waved goodbye
to Enzo and he nodded. He looked so cool and he didn't
even have to try. I nodded to him as well, because to not
do so would have been rude.

As I reached the top of the hill to Marie's house on foot,
I noticed how the sky above me was so different than
the day of Dad's funeral. Now it was breathtakingly blue
and clear for miles in every direction. The thick line of
trees and bushes cleared at the hilltop and I spotted her
house sitting at the opening of a field. I trekked across
the driveway and leaped over three steps on her front
deck, opening the screen door, checking if the door was
locked without making too much of a ruckus. It hadn't
been locked after Catherine and I left, meaning she hadn't
noticed it was open. I turned the knob and carefully slid
open the door. A disheveled Marie stood at the entrance
of the kitchen in a faded yellow bathrobe. She looked up
at me incredulously as I entered.

"Ian, good morning," she said. "I was wondering
where you two wandered off to. Did you go to the convenience store down the street?" She watched me step
inside and paused for a moment, expecting Catherine to
walk in as well. I closed the door behind me.

"No," I said.

"Where's your sister?"

"She's gone home."

"I see." She looked down.

"She couldn't stay," I said. "And she was so excited
about meeting everyone today, but unfortunately she
couldn't change her flight back to Orlando."

Marie sighed. "Well, I'm glad you decided to stay."

"I'll be taking the bus back on Sunday afternoon."

"Perfect," she said, then wandered into the kitchen and started a fresh pot of coffee.

I stood in the opening between the living room and kitchen, unsure of what to do or say next. Although Marie was my aunt, she was also a complete stranger. Neither of us knew a thing about the other, but hopefully that would be different by the time I left on Sunday.

"So, Ian, while you're here I want you to act as if this is *your* house." She smiled. "Can I get you anything?"

I took a deep breath and exhaled loudly to release the anxiety floating in my head. "There's one thing," I said.

"Sure, what would you like?"

"It's an answer to a question."

"Shoot." She started organizing items on her kitchen countertop as I spoke—jars, tins, and containers which had been haphazardly moved in yesterday's mad dash to get out of the house and meet Catherine and me at the cemetery.

"As far as you can remember, was there ever a gold pocket watch that belonged to your father, to the Daly family, actually, and was passed down from generation to generation?"

Marie stopped arranging and appeared deep in thought. She even silently mouthed the words *Gold pocket watch* to herself to help jog her memory. Then she shook her head. "No, not that I recall."

CHAPTER 9

THE MORE I THOUGHT ABOUT IT, I decided Dad's pocket watch had probably been lost in one of our moves. I had certainly misplaced many of my own belongings over the years—keepsakes from the past and toys I thought I never could've lived without. Mom found humor in our compulsion to wander, saying *we move around like a bunch of gypsies.* And she was right. She never shied away from the topic, yet our stay in Florida was still a touchy subject. I never brought it up to anyone because finding a reasonable explanation for what happened was impossible. The lies were much easier to tell.

Mom made the decision to leave Florida on a balmy night before New Year's. My bedroom window had been open for a breeze. Not long after midnight, she opened my door and flicked on the light.

"Wake up! We're leaving. Tomorrow," she said. "Start packing, now."

I sat up in bed and rubbed my eyes. "What? Why?"

"Enough is enough. We need to get back to where things make sense, near our family and better schools. We have to get back to Wellbourne."

"What happened?" I said, looking around, expecting the house to be on fire. "Where's Dad?"

She laughed. "I have no idea where your father is, but we're leaving."

Her red, swollen eyes indicated she hadn't slept, but had spent hours busily rolling fragile items in old newspapers, filling cardboard boxes, and drinking large quantities of coffee. We had moved at least a dozen times, whenever Mom got bored and needed a change, or there was some kind of problem with our landlord, and to be honest there was something exciting about it all. For me, the physical act of moving had become as routine as spring-cleaning. Once I was out of bed and able to comprehend what was happening, I helped take down what made the house ours. We worked all night and at dawn she called her family to wire her the money to rent a truck. Not even twenty-four hours had passed by the time we finished packing the truck. It was some sort of record.

"Are you ready to go?" she called from the driver's seat as I latched the rear door and fastened a padlock. She turned the key and started the engine. "We got to go. Get in."

"Where's Dad?" I asked, climbing into the passenger seat.

"I don't know. We can't wait around here all day. He'll be up when he's up." She pressed the horn. "I always wanted to do that, like a real trucker," she said, grinning. "Now, let's get the hell out of here."

"Did we lock the front door?" I asked.

"Yes, and that reminds me," she said, rolling down the driver's-side window and chucking the keys into the plastic mailbox. "Keys dropped off. Well, that's done. We didn't need the goddamn deposit anyway."

Our first day on the road ended midway through Georgia and then exhaustion set in after sunset. I caught myself dozing off in the front seat. I wasn't able to help Mom with the driving because I hadn't started the process of getting a learner's permit yet, but I vowed to stay awake and keep an eye on her. My head kept dropping slowly to my chest and then I'd snap out of it, seconds before it was too late. Each time I jerked awake, I'd look at Mom to make sure her eyes were still open and we were still safely in our lane. The lines on the road flashed under the car hypnotically and my vision blurred. Soon the road grew so desolate we saw no other cars for hours.

Time dragged on and I grew anxious wishing we'd cover more ground faster. As we drove farther north the ground rippled into hills and mountains, the air cooled, and the humidity dropped. Dark hills surrounded the car like walls on both sides, closing in on us like a cage, and the roads themselves began to twist and turn.

"We're going to pull over soon," said Mom, yawning. "I'm exhausted and I don't know how much more I can go."

"Okay, Mom," I said. "I saw a sign a few miles back for a rest stop. I'm sorry I can't do some of the driving."

"Don't worry about it. We don't need to stop long, just enough for me to rest my eyes."

The rest stop was empty except for two idling eighteen-wheelers and a man and woman with a station wagon walking their German shepherd in the dim streetlights. Mom parked and cut off the engine. She rolled down her window and leaned against the side panel so she could feel the breeze on her face. She motioned for me to put my window down as well and then I leaned back in my chair.

"Get some sleep. I'll wake us up in about an hour," she said with her eyes shut.

She fell asleep quickly. Her breathing was low and heavy, and with her head tilted she snored. I couldn't sleep. I was too worried about something bad happening to us at the rest stop. I turned from one side to the other, shifting myself in the leather seat, trying to reposition my feet by the dashboard, but nothing helped. Every time Mom had stopped for gas I bought a soda, and even though my body felt exhausted, the sugar and caffeine kept me on edge. But I had to be on edge. I had to be there for her and couldn't let my guard down. I was the only one who could help her. I tipped my head to the right and saw the stars unpolluted by city lights, thousands of them like splattered white paint across a dark canvas. Even with the windows down for fresh air, the inside of the truck was humid and the windshield fogged up. I watched the occasional car drive in, park, and people get out to use the bathroom or vending machine.

After about an hour Mom sat up abruptly. "All right, that's enough," she said. She put her long blond hair up. "Did you sleep any?"

"Sure," I said.

"Good. We'll be there soon . . . making great time."

She started the loud engine and popped it into drive. She directed the truck back onto the highway, turning the wheel like the helm of an old ship. Our top speed was only fifty-five miles per hour and the truck gave everything it had. We drove without speaking for a few moments, but I was too strung out for long silences.

"So, what now?" I asked.

"We drop our stuff off at your grandmother's. Stay

a week or so, and then we'll find a place in Wellbourne."

"But then what?"

"Well, you enroll in school and we go back to how things were before," she said. "We're survivors. I'll tell you one thing: you are getting so many wonderful life experiences that none of your friends will ever have. Don't worry about all the rest of it. I always find a way to make it work."

I smiled.

"I'll find some place in town, low-rent, and I'll fix it up and it'll look great. If I'm good at anything, it's making something out of nothing. You know that. It will all work out. And just think, you'll be back with Scott and your other friends again. Aren't you excited about that?"

"Of course I am."

Mom turned the radio on and searched for a new station through the static.

"When do you think Dad's coming up to meet us?" I asked.

She kept her eyes fixed on the road. Discussing our new life kept her energized, but once I brought up Dad she seemed to recoil. "How should I know?" she said.

I don't know why I did it, but I laughed. "But really, what is he going to do?"

"If there's one thing I can say about your father, he's a great salesman. A talker. Knows exactly what to say to anybody to get what *he* wants."

We survived the long night and finally arrived at my grandmother's house in Fairfall Valley. Mom steered the truck into the muddy driveway and I waved at my grandmother, who was rocking anxiously on her front porch. She was shorter than Mom but they looked alike. Her features were rounded off from old age and a big pair of bifocals rested on the bridge of her nose. Her hair was short and gray, and she wore a long skirt and white blouse. Her hands were crossed.

"For heaven's sakes, it's about time you two made it," she said. "I was going to ask your uncle to call the state police, make sure you two hadn't wrecked or got lost."

"Nope, we made it safe and sound," said Mom.

My grandmother pulled herself up slowly and walked over to greet us in the yard. I hugged her and Mom stood beside us checking her watch. She was concerned about returning the truck. Being late incurred extra charges.

"You've grown since I last saw you, Ian," my grandmother said. "You don't have much of a tan. Did you stay inside all day down there?"

"I told you all about it already," said Mom. "Those kids in Florida barely leave their houses. They sit inside the air-conditioning all day. That's one of the reasons we couldn't wait to get back."

"Oh, yes, I recall you saying something about that. Hopefully Ian won't be too behind in school."

"He's fine," said Mom, abruptly.

"Good. I've heard things about those Southern schools."

"He's fine."

"That's one positive in this situation."

"So, where can we start unloading everything?" asked Mom.

"I've cleared a space in the garage, you'll notice when you get back there."

"Thanks again," said Mom. "It'll only be until I rent us a place."

"Sure, whatever you say," my grandmother replied, nodding. "I have to call the rest of the family and let them know you arrived." She went inside while Mom and I returned to the truck.

"Could you take off the padlock and start unloading the boxes? I'll be right back. Do the small stuff and I'll be back to help with the furniture."

"Sure, Mom," I said. "Where are you going?"

"I have to talk to your grandmother about something. Nothing for you to worry about."

I started carrying the boxes labeled *Kitchen* into the area of the garage reserved for us. The space was dusty and giant cobwebs hung in the corners. Everything smelled musty from decades of wet winters and degrading cardboard boxes. A faint odor of kerosene lingered from old space heaters. I made multiple trips to the truck, stacking boxes of similar sizes on top of one another, trying to be efficient, when I heard hushed voices, agitated yet muffled, from a door leading into my grandmother's house. They assumed they were alone. I set down the boxes I had been holding and brought my ear to the door.

"This is a fine old mess you got yourself in," said my grandmother.

"You don't have to tell me what I already know."

"Well, sometimes I wonder what goes through your head."

"What's that supposed to mean?"

"It's been one thing after another with him. I told you not to do it, but now look at all of this," said my grandmother. "And now what?"

"What do you want me to say, Mom? That I wish I could take it all back? That all the shit over the years never happened? That I'm not here begging for your help?"

"All those strange letters," said my grandmother. "I knew there was something wrong with him. None of his family even came to your wedding, and in a Protestant church, no less?"

"He told me he'd been disowned by his family. He wanted a different life."

"What kind of man does that? But really, what are you going to do? What about the boy?"

"What I always do, Mom—survive."

Suddenly they both paused. I imagined they could hear my breathing, as much as I tried holding my breath to avoid being caught. They probably sensed my presence within that pure quiet that highlights even the most insignificant background noises, the kind your brain normally ignores. I quickly picked up the box I'd set down and walked in, pretending I had just come upon them.

"Good, you're here," said Mom. "Change of plan. We're leaving as soon as we finish unpacking."

CHAPTER 10

BEFORE THE GUESTS ARRIVED for the impending family gathering in honor of my father, I sat down with Marie at her kitchen table. She was taking a short break from preparing the house. Her fresh-brewed coffee steamed from the pot as she poured it, and she removed two vacuum-packaged danishes—cherry with vanilla frosting—from the cabinet. The point was for us to bond. I'd be lying if I said sharing was easy for me, and when our conversation eventually started I only shared innocuous details, things any person off the street would know about me and my family. I explained how we had left Florida rather quickly in late December because Mom was anxious to settle back in our hometown of Wellbourne, and how a few months later Dad had booked his temporary apartment in Albany simply to facilitate a new job search. The employment market in upstate New York was horrendous and finding a decent position in Albany was the only way he could support our family. Every word rolled off my tongue as if rehearsed, not that it had been, but I started hearing Mom's voice in my head as I said it. I let it do the talking for me.

I told Marie that Mom and I had returned to our lives back in Wellbourne quite seamlessly. We'd rented a place on West Street, rather than in the affluent section where we used to live and struggled to make rent each month, but Marie didn't know that. West Street ran up a hill, one of the highest elevations in Wellbourne besides the mountains that circled the valley. Unlike the fancy Colonials on the other side of town, where snobs like Eveline Ryan lived, West Street was a row of decrepit houses. Homes were left to the elements, overtaken by weeds, branches, mud, and rodents, until one heavy layer of snow too many cracked their frames and they eventually collapsed. I passed two of those fallen homes on my way to school every day, a sad junkyard of wood and shingles.

I will always remember how Mom presented our new house to me at night, so I couldn't get a good look. Moonlight reflected down a steep driveway leading to a garage—an old barn, really—which I presumed would support the weight of a car if we ever bought one. The house was a deep green, which Mom clarified was evergreen, but much of the paint had chipped off onto the dead landscaping. She had asked the landlord for a key earlier in the day, so we unlocked the front door and walked inside. She pulled out a flashlight and we noticed a pile of dead leaves in one corner of what I assumed was the dining room. Built sometime at the beginning of the last century, the house slanted to the right and the floorboards creaked and groaned with each step. Its foundation was literally old stones piled on top of each other, like a crumbling Civil War fort.

Old latching cabinets hung in the kitchen, which Mom said she loved. A narrow staircase curved upstairs. There were two small bedrooms and a bathroom upstairs with thick gaps between the wooden floorboards. I could look through them to see the living room downstairs. In the bathroom there was a gigantic porcelain tub. The ceiling on the second floor was low and I realized that people were much shorter a century ago. Mom and I weren't that tall so the low ceilings were no bother. I would feel sorry for anyone over six feet who visited. If my old friend Scott Young would come to visit, he'd have to walk around upstairs with his head tilted to one side. Not that I'd invite him.

Regardless of its state, I told Mom that it was a fine house and I couldn't wait for us to move in. I kept having dreams of the house collapsing around us. I couldn't tell Mom about those dreams, of course. She wanted to move in as soon as possible and any reservations from me would make the entire process more stressful. She had already dealt with so many obstacles.

I didn't share any of the memories about my house with Marie. I only described Wellbourne and the renting of our new house in a way to ensure that she understood the good choices Mom had made, how she was a hard worker and always put everyone's needs before her own. The Daly family hadn't met my mother yet, and I didn't want them to have a bad impression if that day ever came.

I did tell Marie that the move had been difficult for all of us and how Mom getting her old job back at Farina's helped ease the transition. Farina's was a restaurant where she had previously worked for years, so I wasn't sharing anything that wasn't already common knowledge. The restaurant served American-style cuisine: steaks, pot roast, hamburgers, and sandwiches. Mom had called the manager as soon as we arrived back. Apparently, another waitress was recently fired for skimming cash out of the register and Mom was a shoe-in. They couldn't pass her up. She was the best waitress in Wellbourne. No one ever complained about overcooked steaks or waited too long for a refill when Mom was on the floor. People from all over Wellbourne requested her section and the manager loved her because she vacuumed, scrubbed the grease off the walls, finished the side work other waitresses hated doing, and even scrubbed the toilets in her downtime.

When I was ten I used to meet Mom for lunch at Farina's every day in the summer. No matter where I was or what I was doing, I'd meet Mom at noon exactly. I'd order a hamburger and fries and Mom made sure it was ready at the exact moment I arrived. The hamburgers were usually burned but I smothered them in ketchup. The fries at Farina's, on the other hand, were perfect. They were never flabby or mushy. Cut from fresh potatoes, they were fried to a golden-brown crisp. The pickles were also my favorite, and Mom knew it, so she had the cook pile extra on the side of the plate, enough individual spears to actually rebuild the original cucumber they had been sliced from.

She was working whenever I visited, but carved out time to sit with me in one of the wooden booths with red vinyl cushions. She'd light a cigarette and just talk, outlining her plans for the house, or what she wanted to do over the weekend. Occasionally, she was forced to stand up to greet new customers or check on tables. Sometimes the men at the bar, *the regulars,* she called them, treated her like she was their personal slave. Drunk by noon, they made rude comments, and tapped their empty glasses on the bar to get her attention. She said they were mostly alcoholics and degenerates who came in every day and spent their entire paycheck. She had to put up with their shit and they rarely left a good tip. Sometimes, when they cackled and asked her to grab a bottle from the bottom shelf because they were *the coldest,* or commented about how they liked the way she blew foam off the top of their beers, I wanted to be bigger and stronger so I could beat their faces in until they apologized and spit out their own bloody teeth.

These details were also left out of my tale to Marie. She didn't need that level of access. Once I finished talking I glanced up. Above Marie's head, hanging on the wall, was a family photograph I'd seen when we first arrived the night before, but didn't feel it was my place to ask about. She noticed me examining the frame and decided to preemptively fill me in.

"That's my baby boy Brandon, although he's not much of a baby anymore," she laughed. "And that's his wife Chelsea and their baby girl Jessica. They took that picture a few years ago; Jessica is going into kindergarten now. They live in Baltimore."

"I see." I nodded quietly because I didn't want to sound like a phony. Marie lit up when talking about her family, so I bit the end of my lip and let her keep going. The truth was, they were also my family, my cousins to be exact.

"Brandon joined the Navy after high school, served his four years as a mechanic and took the same kind of job when he got out. Don't ask me about it, I'm utterly clueless with that stuff." Marie looked at me incredulously. Apparently I had snickered at something she said without realizing it. "What? What did I say?" She wanted to be in on my joke, although I hadn't really made one.

"Nothing," I said.

"Come on, tell me."

"The fact that a man in our family served in the military."

I had briefly considered joining the Army. Whenever I closed my eyes and thought about my future I saw nothing, so at least the Army would keep me busy. They paid for everything, sent you all over the world, and their daily workouts would be as satisfying as anything I ever did at the Wellbourne Boxing Club. My only hang-up with joining the military was the possibility I might actually have to fight or kill someone. There'd come a day when I'd be handed a loaded rifle and ordered to kill a man I'd never met, an individual who like me was just trying to find his way in the world. I had no doubt these thoughts meant I was a coward, but I could live with that. Mom always said I was a pacifist anyway, as harmless as a fly. Men in my family weren't that bold.

"What I mean is," I interjected, not wanting to admit to Marie how I'd assumed all Daly men were draft dodgers and cowards, myself included, "my mother said Dad avoided Vietnam after some accident. There were two versions I heard: one that he fell out of an ambulance while volunteering as a paramedic, and the other that he crashed a motorcycle."

"Yes, that's half true. Thomas avoided the draft, but he never volunteered as a paramedic. He had a plate put in his leg after a car accident. Thomas and a young lady he was dating at the time—I can't remember her name— were found unconscious after hitting a tree, a pint of Wild Turkey wedged under his leg . . . What was her name, was it Michelle? Melissa? One of those, I can't recall."

"How old was he when that happened?"

"Seventeen, I'm pretty sure."

"I see."

"Now, your father's high school friend Frank wasn't so lucky. He was drafted and killed in action."

I had never heard about this friend named Frank before, but then again there were never any words about his other women either.

"I'm sorry, Ian."

I looked back up at Marie. "For what?"

"I take it there are quite a few things you don't know about your father. He always kept to himself, but from what I'm hearing now, it got worse over the years."

"I guess so." I pretended that years of estrangement hadn't bothered me, but since arriving in New Brimfield my mind was overloaded. Reconciling the details and piecing everything together felt like I was trimming old 35mm film, splicing together the true parts and casting the lies into the trash.

Marie stood up and pushed her chair into the table. The wooden legs scratched across the linoleum floor. "Excuse me for a moment, I need to get something," she said, walking into the living room and down the hallway before disappearing into her bedroom.

I stood up as well, picked up the two empty coffee mugs and set them carefully in the metal sink to be helpful. When I turned around Marie stood there with a thin white box in her hands.

"I've had this in my things for a long time. I was never quite sure what I wanted to do with it, but I've figured it out," she said. "Go ahead, open it."

"What is it?" I asked, gently shaking the box.

"Just open it and find out."

The box was secured with a small strip of clear tape. I gently broke it by running a finger through the seam and raised the top to reveal a rectangular piece of multicolored wool.

"What is it?" I asked, lifting the wool from the box. She lifted one end while I held the other.

"It's a scarf," she said. "The pattern is called a tartan. It belonged to my father before he died. Your grandfather."

"Seriously?"

"Yes," she said.

She draped it around my neck. I never wore scarves because they were always so itchy, but this one was soft. The pattern of crisscrossing lines—yellow, red, blue, and white, each of varying thicknesses—reminded me of the argyle socks I saw old men wear when they did yardwork. A strip of white silk was sewn onto one end of the fabric with the manufacturer's name, my family name of *"Daly"* in quotations, a small blue-and-red crest with two dragons, an object resembling a Viking's helmet, and a swan. I held it up to my nose and it smelled like cedar.

"I want you to have it because it symbolizes the Daly family," she said. "Winters get real cold in New York and having only returned from the tropics six months ago, you need a good scarf."

"Tell me about it," I said, recalling my wintry walk with Eveline. "Thank you."

Where my father was involved, disappointment typically followed. I'd grown so used to that feeling that receiving the scarf made me uncomfortable. Satisfied, but uneasy, like I was waiting for the other shoe to drop.

"How did he die? My grandfather," I asked.

Marie said the last person to have seen him alive was my father. The two finished lunch at a diner in New Brimfield, one that had subsequently gone out of business and was demolished to make space for a new post office. He dropped my father off at the house and drove back to work, but on the road he had a massive heart attack that killed him instantly. She said my father was never the same. He was only fifteen. I wanted to be able to say that I had no concept of what it must've felt like for him, but I did.

I was sad about losing my father, but also frustrated with the entire situation. I was angry with him, and then I felt guilty for being so selfish. To make matters worse, I waited anxiously for an intense sorrow to come, the kind that accompanied the loss of a loved one. I had yet to shed one tear over him. Everyone else had cried but me and I didn't know why. I found myself trying to will it, but instead I experienced a steady numbness, like the thrumming of an empty ice machine.

The scarf box was still in my hand and as I went to set it down on an end table, I noticed there were also two old photographs inside. In one, a young woman—clearly Marie—posed in front of the border sign at the New York and Massachusetts crossing. She wore a white dress with a deep red belt. The sun shone on her face and I could almost smell the rich soil and the oak trees around her. In the picture, young Marie appeared delighted.

I suspected that was the true purpose of pictures: recalling honest moments of happiness.

The other photograph was a vertical portrait of a serious-looking man in a military-issued green uniform. I couldn't tell whether it was the Army, Navy, Air Force, or

Marines. He looked like a great man—a hero, in fact. He may've been a distant uncle. There was also a chance he was Marie's husband, whom she had yet to discuss.

"Are these yours?" I asked.

"Oh, I'm sorry," she said, lifting the two photographs. "I forgot that I put those in there."

There was no telling why Marie hadn't given the scarf to her own son. Maybe he had enough family keepsakes to fill a warehouse, or perhaps she had set it aside to give her brother Thomas on the day he decided to reconnect? Either way, she gave me the scarf but took the two photographs from the box.

Soon her guests would arrive and then she wouldn't be able to share so freely about Dad. I didn't know who was coming over, but I did understand how there were certain topics she'd likely have to avoid. No one was quite as eager as I was to get to the bottom of my father's life. Marie stood up and started grabbing napkins and paper plates from a cabinet beside her stove. I wasn't prepared to divulge anything further about my family and I certainly wasn't going to touch on the recent events of my life—what happened with Eveline, Rick, or Scott, for instance. Thinking about Scott, specifically, was like cutting open a scab. There was so much more, so much history between us. Before my family moved to Florida, he had been my very best friend.

CHAPTER 11

SCOTT YOUNG'S MOM HAD WORKED in Wellbourne's only textile factory for as long as I'd known him. We first met in kindergarten when Mom dressed me up in a bow tie on the first day of school. Boys in class gave me a hard time about it, but Scott sat with me at lunch anyway. The other boys were too busy drawing up the new social order that would be in place for years to come. Scott had always been taller than I. Before we moved to Florida he towered over me by a good six inches, but he was skinny as a rail. He carried himself in a withdrawn and curled-up manner, as if always bracing for impact. He had a gentle way about him.

Back in elementary school, Scott started taking karate classes at the Wellbourne Recreation Center. I begged Mom to let me do it too, but I didn't tell her about Scott. I didn't want her to think I was trying to follow in his footsteps. I remember how frequently I stopped by his house after school to watch him prepare for class in his pressed white gi, covered in badges with Japanese lettering and tied together with a matching belt, which reminded me of Mom's terry cloth robe. During these sessions I'd sit back and watch him chew on pretzel rods in his uniform, a barefooted warrior, a honed weapon trained in the secret arts of the Orient. Eventually Mom caved and said I could take eight classes of karate, because she had found a coupon in the newspaper, and that Dad had to drive me every week because she worked extra shifts.

As part of our routine, Dad dropped me off at the recreation center and waited across the street in the Wellbourne Tavern. He said it was easier than driving all the way back home, sitting in front of the television for fifteen minutes, and getting back in the car to pick me up again. I was also relieved he decided to wait across the street so he wouldn't get sidetracked and forget me altogether, except he kept arriving later and later for pickup. Our sensei Terry said it wasn't a problem, but I could tell he was just trying to be nice. He'd finish stacking chairs, piling up gear, and rolling the freestanding heavy bags to one side of the room, and notice me still waiting for my father. Terry would wait with me before turning out the lights. He'd ask if my father remembered what time class ended and I'd say yes, that it was probably bad traffic or an emergency at home, but that excuse would only go so far.

One night Dad stumbled through the front door and kicked over a rack full of pamphlets about the center's summer programming—arts, crafts, sports teams, those types of activities. Terry made a comment about it and Dad told him to *go shit in your hat*. Dad's head was hunched over the steering wheel on the drive home and he scrunched his eyelids, complaining about the brightness of everybody's headlights and how nobody knew *how to fucking drive anymore*.

That weekend Mom told me I couldn't go to karate anymore. I was worried that Dad had upset Terry and got me banned from ever taking the class again. I even prepared a story about how Dad was acting the way he did because of a diabetic attack, but Mom said it was because we owed him money. Terry had called and told her we hadn't paid for my last four classes. She was so embarrassed that I was never allowed to go to his class or to the recreation center again.

The hardest part was explaining to Scott why I wouldn't be in class anymore. Not that Scott had stuck with karate either. He quit about three months later, but he didn't give me a hard time about dropping out when I did. Scott's indifference to the details of my personal life is what solidified our friendship. Back then I believed we'd be best friends for the rest of our lives, yet the slow dissolve began once my family left for Florida. Repairing what had already been lost was impossible. As I came to think about it more, though, how many people have the same best friend for their entire lives? Not many.

Scott did make an effort to visit and reconnect after Mom moved us onto West Street. We'd been back from Florida only a couple of weeks. I considered it a good sign; we'd be able to pick up where we left off. Nothing would be different. One afternoon he unexpectedly knocked on my front door and I was shocked to see him.

"Are you back for good?" he asked.

"I think so." I waved him into the house. Mom had already spruced up the inside and arranged her stuff just so, but it still had a long way to go.

"Hello, Mrs. Daly."

"Why, hello, Scott!" Mom said. "Nice to see you again. You got taller."

I rolled my eyes. I'd never be as tall as Scott, nor did I

particularly care. It bothered me how obsessed everyone was with height, as if you were doomed to failure in life unless you reached a minimum of six feet.

"Thanks, Mrs. Daly."

She flashed a flirty smile and wandered off.

Scott didn't ask about Dad or why he wasn't living with us. He knew me well enough not to ask about my family. That's what I liked most about him. We had a benign conversation about the weather and what I did with my free time. I explained to him that the heat in Florida was disgusting and how I'd rarely gone outside because the sun used to char my skin. He asked about Florida girls and I told him they were beautiful but not very interesting. I also briefly mentioned I had started going to the Wellbourne Boxing Club, but I didn't dwell on it. I still wasn't sure how I felt about the gym and whether it would last much longer.

"I've been hanging out with Rick Sharp a bunch," he said.

"Rick Sharp?" I was shocked. Rick was older than us, a junior who had failed at least one grade and, from what I remembered, a total sociopath. Not even in my wildest dreams would I have imagined a friendship blossoming between them. "Rick Sharp? How did that happen?"

"Well, it's kind of funny, actually. When you left I started sitting next to Rick in algebra and let him copy off my midterm exam. I had no clue if he could do the math or not, but what the hell, right? He got a couple of Bs and the next thing I knew he was inviting me to parties out in the country."

"Weren't you worried he was using you?" I asked. My memories of Rick, stories I'd heard through the rumor mill years ago, came to the surface. "Wasn't he the guy who used to piss in a plastic cup and pawn it off as beer at parties?"

"No way, man. Rick isn't like that. Hey, I'm sure you could come along. He'll probably remember you and you could tag along to a party with me, if you want."

"Maybe."

Scott lit up with a brilliant idea. "Are you busy now?"

"Not really, I—"

"Great! Let's go now. His house isn't far, we can walk."

Rick Sharp's house had blue vinyl siding. One end had been built into the side of a sloping hill, but the concrete foundation kept it all in place. Scott pressed the lit-up doorbell with his thumb. He was so excited, but I was dragging my feet. As we'd been walking there I tried to bring up excuse after excuse about why it wasn't a good time. I couldn't understand why someone who grew up in such a nice house, in a seemingly perfect neighborhood, could be so unbalanced. Rick was the kind of guy who'd intentionally swerve his car to hit a cat crossing the street. He took pleasure in the pain of others.

Loud music blared from inside the house and someone turned it down before we heard footsteps.

"How long are we staying again?" I asked.

"Not sure yet. Just chill, man."

I realized that Scott's plan was to parade me around like livestock at the county fair. His status at school had likely surged once he started spending time with Rick, cruising around town and making appearances at upperclassmen parties in the woods. But now I was back in Wellbourne and we needed Rick's blessing before our friendship could go back to how it had been. Before Rick got his claws into him.

After a few clicks of the dead bolt, the front door swung wide open revealing a middle-aged woman with curly blond hair and a bubbly disposition. She reminded me of a flight attendant and wore skintight blue polyester workout pants with a black sports bra. Clearly she had been exercising. Her skin glistened and beads of sweat dropped down her cleavage. As mothers in town went, she was probably one of the most attractive I'd seen.

"Oh, hey, Scotty!" she said, smiling. Her teeth had been bleached. "I'd give you a hug but I was doing my workout tapes."

"That's fine, Mrs. Sharp."

She patted Scott's back instead and then slid her hands down the small of his back. Mothers loved Scott for some reason I couldn't understand, maybe because he was no real threat?

Once she was finished with Scott, Rick's mom turned and studied me. She stood in place for a moment, her right hand on her hip.

"I'm sorry, this is Ian," Scott said, pointing to me. "He's one of my old friends who just moved back to Wellbourne. I'm bringing him to meet Rick. They are really going to hit it off."

"Of course they will. Everybody loves my little Ricky," she said. "Ian, eh? Nice to meet you."

Before she could put me in a sweaty bear hug, I stuck out my arm and extended my hand for a shake. She glanced at my hand and smiled.

"Yes, Mrs. Sharp, I'm Ian Daly."

She shook my hand vigorously with her warm and

moist one, fluttering her eyelashes. "Daly, you said? Wait a minute, I know your father, Thomas," she said. "How is he? Is he back up in Wellbourne?"

"He's good. Not in town yet, though. He's wrapping things up down in Florida."

"Really? I was wondering if something had happened between your mommy and daddy," she giggled. "Old Tommy. I remember going to one of his New Year's parties at the Radiant, when he was a manager there, years before you were born, I think."

She had this reminiscent look in her eyes as she went on about Dad, how great his parties were, how funny he was, how much everybody in town had a good time with him. She described a man I'd never met. By the time Dad came home to us he was usually quiet, irritable, and slept all day, as if in hibernation. He was either an unbridled flame that burned so hot it couldn't sustain itself for long, or a depleted version of himself, needing to recharge.

"No one was a better time. Tell him I say hi," she said, smirking. "Anyway, sorry to hold you boys up, Rick is downstairs in the basement."

She led us through her living room—the glass coffee table was pushed to one side for her exercises—and pointed to a narrow set of stairs in the kitchen beside the refrigerator leading to the Sharp family basement. The subterranean room was half-finished, with a light-brown carpet like a beaver's pelt. The matching couch and chair were green tweed with hardwood trim and must've been one of the first pieces of furniture they ever bought. Rick was sitting arrogantly in the middle of the couch, clutching a video game controller, glaring at the screen with his mouth slightly open, contemplating his next tactical move. Scott and I stood in place and watched him for a moment until he paused the game.

"What the hell do you want?"

Scott stepped forward. "Hey, Rick."

Rick locked his fingers behind his head and stretched indifferently.

"My old buddy Ian is back in town. I told you about him. He's cool and I wanted him to meet you."

Rick gave me a fist bump, the first in my lifetime.

"Your Mom let us in," I said, trying to break the ice. "You've got a nice house."

"Who, that old slut?" he chuckled. "She's been hopping around up there for hours and it's getting on my fucking nerves."

Not sure how to react, I smiled, and his face slid from playful to serious.

"You think my mom is a slut?"

"Huh?"

I glanced at Scott, wanting to know what to say or do next, but he was looking to the ground like he often did.

"You think you could fuck my mom?" he asked, as serious as a judge handing down a death sentence, although the topic of discussion was anything but.

The room was silent except for the resonance of bass from his mother's exercise music. I stared at him for a moment, noticing the rage in his eyes, and more than anything I prepared myself for either getting my ass kicked or being humiliated. I didn't want to have sex with his mother, even though I had stared at her sweaty breasts.

"No."

Rick convulsed with laughter. "Oh, man, I'm just fucking with you," he said. "Take a seat."

I leaned into the green armchair and Scott took a seat next to Rick on the frayed couch, closer to Rick than me

"So, you just moved back from Florida?" he asked.

"Yes, a couple of weeks ago."

"Why the hell would anyone want to do that?" he laughed. "I don't know, man, the beach, hot girls, spring break."

"My dad got this job offer in Albany," I explained. "But I really liked it down there. I think I'll move down there once I graduate."

"Cool. Oh shit, I didn't offer you guys a drink. Scotty, do me a favor and grab some cold ones from the fridge?"

Rick's father, Deputy Sheriff James H. Sharp, had an extra refrigerator in his basement full of assorted beer bottles. Apparently Sheriff Sharp bought one twelve-pack a week and left any extras in the basement refrigerator like an island of misfit beers. He also didn't mind that his son had access. Scott returned with three chilled Irish Reds, snapped off the tops with a bottle opener screwed into the wall, and passed them to Rick and me. The thought of drinking in a cop's house made me nervous and I squirmed in my seat, occasionally peering back to the basement door to see if his parents were about to bust us. I tried to imagine what excuse I would give Mom when she got the angry phone call from Sheriff Sharp about her son pillaging his family's beer stores.

Rick nodded at Scott when he handed him the slick amber bottle. "Thanks, dick," he said. "You two like the dark shit or do you drink piss like everyone else?" He laughed again.

I noticed that he got a kick out of everything he said. He was his own stand-up comic. I looked at Scott, who was sipping the Irish Red and staring at the floor, deeply contemplating something. I was the last one to take a sip and felt the liquid slide into my stomach, brisk and refreshing. It's funny how sometimes if you drink something really hot or really cold you can actually feel it travel through the inside of your body. The beer wasn't half bad.

"Good," I said, taking another sip. "Thicker than I've had before, but good."

"Are you talking about the beer or Scott's dick?" Rick said, grinning.

The three of us didn't say anything more for a few minutes. We just sat in place, awkwardly drinking our beers. We resembled a group of old men enjoying some cold ones after a hard day's work, the kind of men we'd likely grow up to be. Each of us would find some blue-collar job in Wellbourne—building or assembling or repairing—and carry on drab lives with nagging wives and ungrateful kids, where our only outlet would be polishing off a six-pack after supper. My mind, dipping into a vat of fermented hops, began to drift when Rick finally opened his mouth.

"So, there's this party on Saturday," he said. "Scotty, why don't you bring Ian here along?"

I noticed the joy and relief in Scott's eyes. He had brought me to his new friend, his handler, and it had gone wonderfully. Rick approved of me and that meant the three of us could hang out together in public, as long as I didn't screw it up somehow. Scott now had the best of both worlds. He was ecstatic. The subdued smirk on his face was really an attempt to hide a wide, toothy smile.

CHAPTER 12

NOT THAT THE DALY FAMILY GATHERING was a formal affair, but I didn't want to appear disheveled, not the first time meeting my new family. A quick shower fixed me up and afterward I sat in the living room watching television in one of Marie's extra-large bathrobes while my only outfit went through the spin cycle. I channel-surfed while she carefully unwrapped plastic packages of deli meat and cheese, mixed vegetables, and fruit to serve as appetizers. She pulled the lids off two different kinds of ranch dip and set everything carefully on a card table in the corner of the room. She also collected extra chairs from around the house and arranged them in semicircles next to the blue sectional couch and recliner. Cans of regular and diet soda were meticulously lined up on the top shelf of her refrigerator.

Neil arrived early and let himself in. He spotted me on the couch wearing Marie's robe and looked on warily.

"I'm washing my clothes before everyone comes over," I explained.

"Oh," he replied, dropping a brown bag on the kitchen table. "Marie, I bought some meatballs, but looks like you've already got one here in your living room." He gestured to me with his chin.

"Oh stop, Neil. The boy didn't bring anything else to wear. It's either that robe or one of my dresses. You prefer that?"

"Who knows, I may have." He chuckled and started pulling items out of the bag.

I hadn't stopped changing television channels since I sat down, a nervous tick probably. Marie didn't have many to choose from, not like the guys I knew back at school whose parents could afford lavish cable packages, yet I still couldn't make up my mind. I had no idea what I was looking for. I finally surrendered and dropped the remote in exasperation, leaving an old kung fu movie from the seventies playing on the screen, a clichéd story of betrayal and revenge where the English voices were dubbed and men possessed an abundance of body hair. Neil unpacked his contribution to the gathering and Marie finalized her spread to an orchestra of bizarre yelping karate chops and tacky jazz music.

Marie eventually asked me to turn down the television volume and I turned it off instead. I hadn't been watching anyway. Having it on was a distraction from thinking about all the new people I was about to meet. At least I knew Marie and Neil, so if the situation with another family member became heated I could always stick behind them. I had really hoped to spend more time with Neil during my stay, being that he was Dad's older brother. Neil became the family patriarch after my grandfather died and I was curious to pick his brain about my father. The problem was, he possessed many of the same qualities as Dad. He didn't want to talk. No doubt a family trait.

An obnoxious buzzing from down the hall indicated

that the dryer was finished with my clothes. I walked toward Marie's bedroom and took a sharp right into the laundry room. After carrying my heap of clothes into her bathroom, I slipped off the robe and hung it on a hook behind the door. Her bathroom was narrow. The shower, sink, and toilet were of a matching avocado color with white tiles that took a faint diamond pattern. The shower curtain was white and a fuzzy sandy-brown lid covered the toilet. My clothes were warm as I put them on, and when I left the bathroom I was ready to face whatever came at me, which got me thinking about my short-lived boxing career.

Closing the space between me to an opponent felt counterintuitive at first, but the truth was it denied them the room to get enough leverage to throw a good punch. Boxing was all about training your body to do the opposite of what it instinctually wanted to do. The more I practiced, the easier it all became. My form improved and soon I could punch the bag without straining my wrist. One of the last nights I went to the gym, Bud assigned me counterpunching combinations on the heavy bag. Every punch had a corresponding number, from one to six, and he asked that I spend three rounds circling the bag and throwing a one-two-slip-two-three, meaning a jab, a right cross, a slip to the right, as if anticipating a swing from my opponent, another right cross, and a left hook to top it all off. Then I had to circle the bag, mixing up my combination with a few jabs to keep my opponent off his game, and repeat the combination again from a new angle. Boxing was all about the angles, he said.

The rounds passed quickly as I circled and stalked the

red, lopsided, heavy bag. My shoulders tightened in the last round and my lungs burned to the point where it was difficult to breathe, but I kept punching because I didn't want to disappoint Bud.

Bud said counterpunching, which entailed the use of timing, speed, and accuracy to beat your opponent to the punch, was the key to being a truly great fighter. In order to be an effective counterpuncher you had to anticipate when your opponent was going to strike, dodge the punch, and simultaneously unleash your own quick response. I realized the same could be said of life. There were people in the world desiring to harm others for no logical reason. And like facing an opponent in the ring, I had to anticipate and react to what *they* might do. I never wanted to be the guy who took it and turned the other cheek. Not anymore.

Once I finished my rounds on the heavy bag, Bud called to me from the ring. He told me to lace up a pair of gloves and find headgear because I was going to work on counterpunching with Enzo.

Somehow his request made me feel nauseated and exhilarated at the same time.

"Really? Are you sure?" I asked. "I'm not sure if—"

"Yes. Yes, you'll be fine." He felt my apprehension, which filled the room like billowing black smoke. "We'll go easy the first time."

Enzo nodded in agreement.

It wasn't that I was afraid Enzo would do something to intentionally hurt me; I was more terrified of looking like a fool.

I finally accepted my fate. I shuffled over to the rickety equipment table and chose a puffy pair of red sparring gloves and black leather headgear that clasped tightly under my chin. An Everlast logo stitched into the headgear would be Enzo's target. The wood floor of the ring shifted and groaned as I stepped along the one-inch padding that covered it, providing some buoyancy for our ankles and joints. Enzo was already warmed up, sweaty and glistening, and even Bud, who had been wearing a chest protector and training mitts, was soaked through his sweatshirt.

For the drill, Enzo would be throwing jabs or right crosses at half speed and I'd have milliseconds to decide whether to duck left or right to avoid getting hit. Once I was comfortable enough with the drill, Enzo would throw faster. Bud said it would prepare me to spar, though I wasn't in a hurry to proceed to the next step.

Enzo shuffled up to me and I didn't move much, which was my first mistake. He started off by throwing a delicate jab, which I easily slipped to the right. He decided to turn up the speed and started throwing jabs and right crosses a little harder and faster. Most of his punches hit me directly in the forehead, but I'd like to say I dodged a few. The drill turned into a constant onslaught of padded red leather colliding with my face. I felt overwhelmed and ashamed, and wanted nothing more than to stop and find any excuse to go home. But Bud had been watching and I didn't want him to think less of me. For some inexplicable reason, I was deeply concerned with his opinion.

Enzo's punches started sneaking between my hands and several caught me square on the nose, clogging everything up like a bad sinus infection. I couldn't breathe and my nose hurt. Sweat trickled down the front of my face, a skin-crawling sensation. I wanted to scratch with my glove but I couldn't without lowering my defenses. Bud ordered us to break for a moment and walked up to me with a piece of wadded paper towel, dabbing my nose and lifting it to reveal blotches of red. The droplets on my face weren't sweat after all—I was bleeding! No one warned me I might bleed.

"Don't worry," Bud said, holding my head up and sticking wads of the paper towel into my nostril like a plug. "This always happens the first time you get punched in the face. The blood vessels and cartilage haven't hardened up yet. You'll survive."

"You all right?" Enzo asked from the opposite corner.

"Yeah, fine. No problem."

Everybody bled the first time, he said. I'm sure Enzo remembered his first bloody nose. But I didn't want to seem weak, so I kept my mouth shut. I secretly hoped Bud couldn't get my nose to clot and that we'd have to finish early, but instead he balled up the soiled paper towel and tossed it in the garbage can beside the ring.

Enzo threw more than he did before, as if he had forgotten my bloody nose, or didn't care. The punches were only half of what he was capable of, but they still hurt like hell. My eyes watered and my nose started to ache. With every punch I felt this twinge of rage. A base and primal feeling surfaced inside me. I subtly opened the space between my gloves to allow Enzo's fists to reach my face more easily. There was something cleansing about the pain. He doubled up his jabs, two to my face, and finished off with a right cross. I stood in place, not moving a muscle. The cartilage in my nose cracked with each punch and I stopped slipping punches altogether. I wanted to hurt, to bleed again, let it all drip down my face and stain my T-shirt. I wanted to hit back too, but that wasn't part of the drill. Enzo, noticing how I had given up on defense entirely, paused for a moment and leaned in close.

"Hey, man, you all right?"

"Fine, why?"

"You aren't moving? Are you hurt?"

Nothing was wrong. I was getting what I needed, what I deserved, and I wanted to see how much more I could take.

"No. Just keep going."

The round ended and Bud ordered us to break. My head ached and hot blood pumped deep into my throbbing skull. I slipped off my sweaty headgear. My head was as heavy as a boulder and I was woozy, but the worst part was my sore neck. Bud and Enzo both said I did well, though I didn't believe them. Enzo had been training with Bud for years and they were so close. I wasn't jealous or anything, though I wondered how many fathers one guy needed. Not to disparage Enzo, but he collected father figures like others did stamps. He had a real father, three brothers who acted like surrogate fathers, and he had Bud at the gym. I felt that enough was enough and it was time to let somebody else take a turn.

CHAPTER 13

DAD FREQUENTLY BRAGGED ABOUT bar fights he'd been in over the years, the *donnybrooks*, he called them. One night I remember he actually came home with a missing tooth and swollen jaw, blood all over his shirt. So when I told him about my nights at the boxing gym over the phone—when he'd first moved up to Albany—I half expected him to be proud, but he wasn't. His reaction was to instead congratulate me on not being gay. "We were all a little worried there for a while," he said, chuckling. I was furious, but only for a moment. I had no right to be angry. Fathers naturally worry about their sons and nothing I did ever put him at ease regarding which way I leaned. He never once saw me on the living room couch with a girl or sneaking one up to my bedroom. The currency needed for being a man in Wellbourne was measured out in pretty young faces.

What really got on my nerves was how every guy in Wellbourne was so obsessed with not being gay. Like how my father and the others believed a man wasn't a man unless he was weathered and engaged in rough activities like football or fixing a car with his bare hands. Homosexuality was a virus that one caught living outside the prescribed vision Wellbourne had for its boys. Sign up for musical theater one time instead of the wrestling team and suddenly they all knew. But why couldn't they do both? None of this was the reason I had started boxing in the first place, of course, but now that I was training regularly I didn't feel more or less manly than I did before. I still couldn't throw a football and if asked to do so, I couldn't pop a hood.

From what I could tell, it was all a bunch of bullshit. Over the months leading up to Dad's death, I started suspecting that many of the certainties I'd grown up with, including how guys I knew in school viewed the world, simply weren't real. They couldn't be, nothing was so cut-and-dried. Rick Sharp was one of the worst offenders and I noticed it the more he spoke.

"What's the matter with you, are you a *faggot* or something?" Rick shouted one night in his basement, over the sounds of his video game, because I'd once again refused to accompany them to a party in the woods.

"Huh?"

Without saying another word, he hunched over and pulled an intricate glass bong from the side of his couch, tucked in next to the wood-paneled wall. The bowl flashed bright orange before he pulled a glass piece up and cleared the white smoke in one breath. He blew it out in my direction and I felt woozy.

"You've got to go," Scott repeated to me on behalf of Rick.

So far I had been giving clever excuses, but my material was running dry and they had persisted.

"Where's this party?" I asked.

"You should've seen this guy a few weeks ago," Rick said, eyes bloodshot, crushing the buttons on his controller. "There's this whore. Monica. Monica, right? What's her name, Scott?"

Scott grew somber and answered in monotone: "Monica. Monica Davenport."

"Oh yeah, big ass, I'd tap it," Rick laughed. "I showed Scottie what to do. Right, Scottie?"

"Yup."

I was confused. Scott had never mentioned her to me before.

"He's the fucking man. I wanted to celebrate with him," said Rick. "She would've been up for us both, but I was busy of course." Rick snickered. Whatever he was shooting at in the video game exploded into a fireball. "Damn, just beat my top score," he muttered to himself.

"So what happened with her, exactly?" I asked, directing my question to Scott because I wanted the real story. Rick seemed to exaggerate everything. Scott opened his mouth to respond but Rick cut him off.

"Damn, Ian, what's your problem, man? I told you, the boy got some ass. Why can't you just be happy for him? What, are you swimming in the pussy?"

"Well, no, not exactly."

Scott suddenly lifted his head excitedly, remembering a chip he held in his back pocket. "Ian wants to hit that new redheaded girl, the hippie chick. Elaine? Is that her name? No. Eveline." He grinned at Rick, yearning for his approval. It made me sick.

Scott knew her name. I don't know why he pretended otherwise.

"Really, Ian? You like that fire crotch? Does the carpet match the drapes?"

"I wouldn't know," I said. "First of all, I don't 'want'

her, and second of all, I never saw her naked. Really, I just think she's irritating, the way she keeps talking to me."

Rick was intrigued. "So you're saying you can't seal the deal?"

"Ian," declared Scott, his tone unwavering, "Rick is a god when it comes to hooking up, seriously. If you want Eveline, he'll show you what to do."

I'd be lying if I said Scott wasn't getting on my nerves too. This wasn't the Scott I knew. He was acting like a starving animal searching the floor for Rick's scraps.

I faked a smile. "All right, Rick, what's the big secret then?"

"Secret?" said Rick, sneering. "No secret. You just party with them and you have to be in the right place at the right time. You might not know this yet, but every girl is looking for an excuse to drop her panties. Simple as that."

"That's it, just stand next to them?" I replied mockingly. "If that was the case I should've been laid a hundred times already."

"Hey!" Rick shouted furiously. "Fuck you, man. Seriously, Scottie, what the fuck did you bring into my house?"

I was shocked at how quickly Rick's mood changed. My face flushed and I thought about how all the progress we'd made as new friends was gone. Rick could take a swing at me, or worse yet, banish me from his house, thereby permanently severing my friendship with Scott. He had that power. He was also much larger and stronger than I was, and capable of inflicting a lot of damage. I should've just kept my mouth shut.

"No, man, it's not like that, sorry," I said, hoping to make amends.

He watched me closely for a moment and then burst out laughing. "I'm just fucking with you. You're too easy. Scott, did you see his face?"

They both laughed at me and I eventually joined in with a fake chuckle. As much as Rick played off his bad temper as a practical joke, there was something genuine about it. I had witnessed true rage before, so I knew. A part of him had held back from reaching a full boil, but there would come a day when all that control was lost. The thought made me uneasy. I couldn't tell Scott I thought Rick was some psychopath ready to lose it at any moment, so I had to accept my situation. I suppose Rick and I had hit it off, though it didn't feel that way. I don't know if he liked me and I didn't quite trust him, but at least the three of us were clear to hang out. As long as I didn't screw it up by running my mouth again.

Days after my visit to Rick's basement I still pondered our conversation. The two of them were still pressuring me to ride along to one of these parties, and sooner or later my declining would cause a serious rift, something I wouldn't be able to mend. I knew how badly Scott wanted the three of us to work out, so I'd try for him. To me it sounded as if their whole purpose of attending these parties was to get off with whatever girl was in the mood that night, which in reality didn't sound half bad. I'd never been with a girl before and as much as Rick tried to brag about Scott's night with Monica—whoever she was—I was fairly certain he still hadn't either. Scott told me everything. He would've told me if he was interested in a girl from school, especially if he got somewhere with her. Rick was just telling one of his stories.

My problem was that I had no other prospects. The

only girl who I kept running into over and over again was Eveline Ryan, and she didn't count because she was brand new to town.

I saw her again one day after school and somehow got trapped into walking her home. Eating pizza with her had complicated everything, and now it was difficult to ignore her. Many of my recollections from that afternoon were fuzzy, except I vividly remembered it being a crisp day. Something about late afternoons in winter were depressing; the darkness came earlier, lips chapped, noses ran, ears were ice cold, and life was frozen in place. Lush trees grew bare, plants withered away to nothing, and bland white steam rose from drafty brick buildings. Nature had its own way of expressing loneliness. Eveline and I strolled west; the descending sun burned my eyes. I had no sunglasses, which was a disappointment because they would've furnished me with a feeling of anonymity.

She gently opened and closed her front door, and chimes attached to the inside doorknob rang like we were stepping into an old lady's gift shop. I expected a vicious dog to come running, but nothing did. The house smelled like scented candles or incense. I wouldn't quite describe it as fancy, but it was filled with aged books, polished antiques, and artwork on the walls. The sort of place I imagined a history professor living in—modest yet intellectual. Her parents weren't home. I found myself a little anxious thinking about what they would say if they walked in to find a strange boy in their house. Or if she had a big, steroid-fueled long-distance boyfriend who'd break down the door and rearrange my face into a rubbery pile of mush. I had learned a few defensive moves at the boxing club—slipping, parrying, and countering—so

I might be able to survive long enough for him to run out of steam and make my escape.

"So this is my house," she said, her arms dramatically extended. "Do you like?" She flashed this flirty grin and my eyes were drawn to the cherry-colored gloss on her lips.

I never realized it before, but her smiles had a calming effect on me, which was strange to admit. As she gave me the tour, I started thinking of excuses as to why I'd have to leave immediately. But I was so nervous I couldn't come up with anything, and besides, I had already told her I had nothing planned, so I was stuck. Mom warned me about these kinds of girls because they trapped guys in a web.

"It's a nice house," I said.

She strutted in front me. I stared at her behind. "Thanks, maybe you can show me *yours* sometime?" she said, spinning around to face me.

"Um, I'd love to, but it's just under a lot of renovation right now. We're barely allowed inside. It just wouldn't be safe."

"I forgot," she said. "Didn't you say your dad is moving back to Wellbourne? Will it be ready by the time he arrives?"

"I just don't know. Maybe." I looked down and around the room, waiting for her to change the subject.

She stepped through her ornate living room and sat down in front of a brown piano, gently lifting the lid. "Come, sit here," she said, patting her hand on the empty space beside her on the bench. "I promised I'd play for you."

I knew we were alone, but I glanced around the room

and peered out the front window to check that her driveway was empty. This guy from Florida told me about his father walking in on his sister on the couch with some random boy. She was topless with her blue jeans rolled down to her ankles. The father slammed the guy against the wall and cracked a few of his teeth before the guy managed to pull up his pants and sprint out the front door. I wondered if Eveline's parents even allowed guests in the house when they were gone. Mom hated it when my friends came over, even when she was home. I think it was just too mentally taxing for her.

I shuffled over to the bench and finally sat down, and my arm brushed against her bare, cool skin.

"This is something I've been practicing for a recital next month," she said, licking the tip of her finger before turning one of the sheet-music pages.

"Play away," I said, shaking my foot and biting my lip.

She started. As soon as I heard the melody, my anxiety melted away.

Eveline's delicate fingers danced across the keys and I closed my eyes. I thought about dark things like the black keys on the piano and the inside of my own eyelids. When I opened them, our eyes met.

"You are so good at this," I said.

She smiled.

I placed my hand on top of hers and felt her muscles, tendons, and bones jostle as she played. She slowed a bit and looked at me questioningly out of the corner of her eye. I kept my hand on top of hers and it was so soft. There had to be something more to life, I thought, something good and honorable, otherwise how could a girl fiddling with a wooden box be capable of producing such beautiful sounds? I wouldn't have ever said that to Scott or Rick, but it's what I believed. They wouldn't have understood anyhow, and they would've called me a *fag*, but it's not like they could force me to believe something different. No one could control the way I saw the world.

She stopped playing and looked at me with her clear blue eyes. She seemed to be moving her face closer to mine, so I kissed her soft lips and it felt right.

She flinched and leaped out of her seat.

"What?" I shouted. "What did I do?"

"We can't do this."

"Do what?"

"This."

"I wasn't doing anything. We weren't doing anything. I was just listening to you play." I sat back down on the piano bench as if nothing had happened. "I swear. I'm sorry. Let's pick up where we left off."

Her initial shock—not to mention her complete physical revulsion toward me—faded as she gazed into my eyes. She clearly needed time to process and think about what I had done; seconds weren't enough time to make judgments, not for a girl like her. I squeezed my fists, bracing for the moment when she'd angrily demand that I *get the hell out* and maybe slap me across the face. She took a step forward and pressed her lips against mine again with such force that our foreheads nearly collided. Our kissing grew longer and deeper as we seemed to wrestle each other across the room and simultaneously drop onto the couch, our kisses unbroken, and my hands sliding up and down her thighs and waist. As if experiencing shock in the heat of an epic battle, I acted in ways I had never expected of myself. Somehow my hand hovered over the button of her jeans and she nodded vigorously and I tugged at it until it came loose.

She slid her whole body close to me and reached down my pants, wrapping her warm fingers around me completely and tugging energetically, moaning lightly between deep breaths. I closed my eyes because it was too difficult to look at what she was doing. Blood traveled to my waist so quickly I felt light-headed and ready to burst. When I opened my eyes briefly, I saw her shirt was off. Her fair skin reminded me of this mother-of-pearl guitar pick I had stolen from my music teacher's desk in the fifth grade. At the time I had wanted it because I liked how the varying shades of white and cream twirled across the surface of the pick, like shells I found on the beach in Florida.

I couldn't explain what prompted me to think of that mother-of-pearl guitar pick, but the next image that flashed across my blood-starved brain was Mom.

I pulled away.

"What? What's wrong?" asked Eveline. Her pale face was now flushed and her clothes were in disarray, revealing different portions of her body

"I'm so sorry," I said. "I can't do this after all. I was wrong. I'm sorry." My stomach churned. This wasn't right. I shouldn't behave this way. I stood up and started to adjust my clothing.

Eveline's bright blue eyes grew red and tearful, and she scrunched herself up on the couch. "What did I do?" she asked, sobbing.

"Nothing. You did nothing. It's just . . ." I didn't know what to say because my mind was occupied with repeating one single phrase to myself until I wanted to puke: *What would she think?* "I'm sorry. I have to go. "

Eveline said nothing.

I stepped off her front porch and ran home.

CHAPTER 14

ONCE MARIE'S GUESTS ARRIVED, all six of us sat down in a lopsided circle in the living room, among mismatched folding chairs and permanent pieces of furniture. No one engaged in nervous chatter. Each person quietly eyed the others and fiddled with slices of cheese or vegetables placed precariously atop mini-plates. I sat on the right end of Marie's couch, partially leaning on the armrest, and I felt disappointed at the turnout. For some inexplicable reason I thought her house would be bustling with activity and we'd have to spill out into the backyard. A large concrete slab in the back with lawn chairs would've accommodated at least an additional ten people.

Around the living room were Marie, Neil, their cousin Glenn, and his uninteresting wife Lisa. The last person in the room was Carla, who had stayed the night with a friend of hers in town and appeared well rested. As the introductions were being made I swiped my hand through the air, an unambitious wave like royalty in public, a signal to Glenn and Lisa that I was glad to have met them but not overly emotional under the circumstances. They smiled back. I surmised that Marie and Neil didn't see much of Glenn around New Brimfield, but he lived close enough to answer their last-minute invitation to honor my father. No one really seemed close. They were all like casual acquaintances, waving at each other from in line at the hardware store or post office, obligated to attend each other's major functions because it was the right thing to do. If given the choice, I doubt most families would actively spend time together, if not compelled by a sense of duty and the shared blood coursing through their veins.

Marie thanked everyone for being there and said how my father would've been happy that we'd come. *God bless his soul*. I don't know if what she said was true, but Neil stood up to make his second trip to the hors d'oeuvres table as she spoke. His mission was to single-handedly consume all of his own meatballs. I questioned Marie's words because it seemed to me that the last thing my father would've ever wanted was for everyone to be in the same room together.

Glenn chipped into the conversation Marie was working so hard to initiate. He decided to provide us all with a little family history. He described how my grandmother Virginia—whose name I only learned for the first time in his story—came from a family of equestrians north of London. They bred and raised the finest high-stepping Hackneys in all of Yorkshire. My grandmother had immigrated to the United States as a young woman and met my grandfather in Brooklyn. Glenn didn't know much about her life after that, except for a twelve-month stay in an upstate New York sanitarium. According to him, it was difficult for her to adjust to the unexpected death of her husband and taking care of three children on her own in a small town like New Brimfield. He said the place where she stayed resembled a resort more than a health facility, but the point of the story was that she got the help she needed. Marie and Neil hadn't shared that story with me and I suspected it was because they were much more sensitive about their mother's story than Glenn, who they only saw sporadically. She wasn't his mother after all.

As I listened, a memory jolted loose, something I hadn't thought of in years, a sensation as jarring as déjà vu. I couldn't recall Dad ever being physically sick, not until the end of his life. Compared to his peers, I'd say his doctor's visits were infrequent. He didn't have diabetes, high blood pressure, or blocked arteries. But Dad hated doctors. The last place in the world he'd want to be was in a damn hospital, but once, when I was six or seven, he got so sick that Mom drove him two hours away and forced him into one. He had no choice but to agree with her. I was very young, so it was difficult to gauge the amount of time he was there. Maybe it had been a month or two.

Mom was forced to pick up even more shifts at work as a result, but she said he'd return to us stronger and healthier than before. Whenever Catherine or I asked what was actually wrong with him, Mom blamed a rare case of pneumonia. And most importantly, no matter what, we couldn't tell anyone he was there. If someone pressed the issue, like a neighbor or a nosy teacher, we'd have to say he was out of town at a business conference.

We all visited Dad one weekend. He gave one of his "grand tours" of the hospital, showing it off like it was Buckingham Palace. He complained about having to share the same floor with *diseased whores and junkies*, not understanding why they couldn't move him to another wing. At first he was wearing a hospital gown, though fortunately the staff permitted him to change into his street clothes—jeans and a sweatshirt—for our visit. The staff was very polite but insisted on being with us throughout the entire visit, watching us intently to make sure we weren't doing something wrong.

Dad led us through an unmarked exit door, which opened to rusty train tracks behind the hospital. His intention was to show us how pennies got flattened on the tracks when a train passed. Catherine was frightened because she was worried that it would cause a derailment and hurt someone. Mom and Dad laughed at her and she stood red-faced by the wall for the remainder of the visit. Dad spent much of his time by those tracks, he told us, smoking and thinking deeply, because the *pain-in-the-ass* staff prevented him from stepping farther than twenty-five feet from the building. He said it had something to do with being contagious, but he certainly didn't seem sick to me. In fact, he kept laughing to himself about being the least sick person in the whole place.

I hadn't thought about Dad's stay at the hospital for years; in fact, I had nearly forgotten it until I heard Glenn talking about my grandmother in the sanitarium.

From the edge of Marie's couch I noticed Carla, who sat across from me, shifting anxiously in her seat. She was waiting to be heard but her patience was growing thin. I thought about how easy it was to reactivate memory, how fascinating to have a story, a name, or even a strong scent, revive something you thought was lost forever. How the eau de toilette Mom kept in the medicine cabinet in our old house reminded me of the nights she curled her hair for date night, with a freshly lit cigarette hanging from one corner of her mouth, or the smell of Dad's musty paperback books in the garage.

But now, all I seemed to think about was the image of disheveled red hair and the rank odor of puke, reviving unbelievable feelings of guilt.

Carla moved her lips silently, warming them up for addressing our group. She seemed to be timing Glenn, waiting for him to take a breath or a sip of water so she could interject. Glenn spoke with a slow drawl, so as soon as Carla's energetic voice piped in everyone snapped back to attention. She immediately went into a well-rehearsed speech about her children, Mark and Ashley. Mark was a champion soccer player and Ashley was passionate about showing animals at the county fair. She said Mark was a "talented young athlete, given the circumstances," meaning growing up without a father. If we learned anything from her lengthy monologue it was how they were both extraordinary human beings. I considered pointing out to her that I had lived with our father my entire life, but was no closer to being any of those things. In his own twisted way, Dad's abandonment probably did Mark a favor.

Mark's athletic gifts struck me as odd, though, and that was one detail that had me questioning Carla all over again. My father was on the lanky side, but about two or three inches taller than I. He had zero muscle mass, poor eyesight, lousy balance, and a severe lack of coordination. Describing him as having a total ineptitude for physical activity was not an understatement. On the other hand, the glorious children Carla described, who allegedly shared part of my DNA sequence, didn't fit that bill. Both Catherine and I were on the same pathetic level as Dad in athletics, so how was Mark so physically gifted? To be fair, the argument could be made that every child develops differently, yet the sad truth we all had to face was that certain undesirable parts of a family's genetic makeup couldn't be diluted.

I watched Carla as she spoke, still wondering if everything she said was a calculated lie. And I tried to imagine what it would've been like if Dad had stayed married to her all these years. My consciousness may have been implanted in a face I never would have recognized in the mirror. I might've had leathery skin and a compulsion to crash other people's funerals. But, even more terrifying, all traces of my sister and me would have been wiped from the genetic lottery. Catherine and I would've never existed, except for perhaps in some parallel universe.

Carla caught me staring at her. "This is certainly a sad day," she said, scanning the room. "Probably the most for you, Ian. Thomas had his faults, but I believe he was a good man. I still remember the day we met." She cracked a smile, subtle and reminiscent.

Neil rolled his eyes from across the room.

"You'll like this story, Ian," Carla said. "We met in high school, New Brimfield High School, the one right next to the cemetery. He was my first crush. We were high school sweethearts, as a matter of fact. He was just so charming, so worldly. Everything he said was always exactly what I wanted to hear."

"This is *my* father you're talking about?" I said.

"Yes, yes, of course," she replied, slightly offended that I had interrupted her. After refocusing, she continued: "We dated all through high school and I knew he was the one. Once we graduated he asked me to marry him. He was so different back then, so full of optimism and drive. I thought he was going to take over the world, and he could've done it too, but nothing ever seemed to work out for him."

Marie smiled at Carla and I couldn't tell if it was out of pity.

I asked Carla about when she first met Dad's family.

"We all went to school together—Marie, Neil, me, and even June—in different grades of course, but he never told me much about his family and we never visited. I remember wondering if he was ashamed of me."

"June?"

Marie lowered her head and addressed me softly: "June was our younger sister, she passed three years ago, from cancer."

"Oh, I'm sorry," I said. "I didn't know."

Carla's eyes had started to well up and she dabbed at them with a tissue. At first I thought that the topic of June had brought tears to her eyes, but really she was still absorbed in her memories of Dad. She kept saying whatever thoughts popped in her head, as if she were alone in the room.

"My mother kept telling me there was something off about him," she said, starting to get choked up. "And to be honest, we were both shocked when he proposed. I don't know if it's what he really wanted. Our marriage was fine those first few years, before he left."

"Why did he leave?" I asked.

Marie put her arm around Carla and decided it wasn't the right time for that question to be answered. "Is anyone hungry? We have plenty of food," she said. "Please, please, help yourselves. Maybe we should all take a break. Anyone need a drink?"

The group stood up simultaneously. Her arm still

draped around Carla's shoulder, Marie led her to a bedroom for some privacy. Glenn joined Neil at the food table for pointless small talk about the previous winter's snowfall in New Brimfield and his boring wife stepped outside to retrieve something from their parked car. I snatched a bright red can of Coca-Cola from Marie's refrigerator and reveled in the sound of gas escaping as I cracked it open. Feeling hungry, I also picked up three different types of cheese cubes and some broccoli with ranch dressing. I returned to my designated seat on the couch and started to enjoy my bounty when I noticed Marie return alone from the bedroom. She stepped in front of the refrigerator and stood on the balls of her feet to retrieve something from the top, stuffed between a ceramic cookie jar and a gigantic box of cereal. Then she slipped out into the backyard.

I followed her outside because I felt curious and had nothing else to do. She was facing the state forest behind the house that sprawled as far as the eye could see. Her yard stretched about fifty yards before running into the thick tree line, a sharply defined border to a foreign land. A long, skinny cigarette hung between two of her fingers and she periodically lifted it to her mouth for a drag.

"What's going on?" I asked.

She turned and flashed me a beleaguered smile. "Nothing, really. Just old wounds."

"I guess that's family, eh?"

She chuckled to herself and took another hit of tobacco. "Well, between you and me, Carla is a little sensitive to begin with, but anyone can figure that out within five minutes of meeting her." Marie peered through the kitchen window to see if anyone was still interested in the food table. "I know this is all a lot to take in over the course of one day."

I nodded.

"Two days ago you wouldn't have even recognized me in the grocery store," she laughed.

Being in New Brimfield felt like an out-of-body experience, a dream that I'd eventually wake up from and shake off. All the revelations about Dad had chiseled away at my impression of him, until I didn't know what to believe any longer. The uncertainty caused my head to spin.

"I'm glad I came," I said.

"Good."

"One thing has been on my mind, though. Why did my father leave town?"

"I never wanted to cast your father in a disparaging light," she said. "But there are other factors involved here. Nothing is ever black and white."

"Like what?"

"What happened with Baby Tommy, of course," she said. "I don't think your father really ever got over it."

"Whose baby?" I asked anxiously.

"One of his babies, a boy. He died."

Marie shared the last story I'd hear about Dad that afternoon. In the late 1960s Dad's friend Frank, who died in Vietnam, was dating a beautiful woman with dark features named Janice Malone. Janice and Frank would regularly meet my father and his young bride Carla for a double date. They were the best of friends and would go out to dinner, the movies, or huddle around the living room for a laugh with a bottle of wine. Over one of those pleasant evenings, Frank told the group he had been drafted. The collective reaction from the group was

one of shock, except for Dad, who reasonably felt relief
at avoiding the draft due to his leg injury. Frank wasn't
shaken by his looming deployment, but he did express
concern over Janice. He pulled my father aside and asked
that he keep an eye on her until he got back.

When Frank left, Janice was devastated. She became
depressed and hardly left the house. Even though Dad
had two young children with Carla—Mark and Ashley—
he set aside time daily to stop in and check on her. One
thing led to another, according to Marie, and his one-
on-one visits became quite a bit more than making sure
the cabinet was full of groceries, or the lightbulbs were
changed. Janice soon discovered that she was pregnant
and, given the time frame, it could've only been my father's. Not surprisingly, Carla didn't take the news well
and my father left her and the children, who were in diapers the last time they saw their father. Dad started living with Janice and the two carried on like they were
reenacting the pages of some trashy romance novel. They
were both young and selfish, explained Marie, and tried
to turn their little fantasy into a way of life.

Janice's baby boy Tommy was born happy and healthy
at seven pounds. The couple was ecstatic and couldn't
believe their good fortune, until one night when they
went to check on Tommy in his crib and noticed he had
stopped breathing. Marie said my father was never the
same. Although the couple was still together, Dad spent
less time with Janice. Many of his nights were now spent
in the Eagle Inn. Not even hearing the news that Janice
was pregnant again months later, this time with their second son, Cameron, could've saved their relationship. Dad
left town shortly after and settled in Wellbourne.

"Tommy is actually buried not far from your father," said Marie.

"What ever happened to Janice?"

"She lives here—in New Brimfield, I mean. Let's just say there's still some bad blood."

C HAPTER 15

THE DALY FAMILY GATHERING ENDED a mere three hours after it began and it felt like another letdown because I had built this grand scenario in my head where the blindfold was finally lifted. That never happened and now it all seemed even more complicated. Carla returned from the bedroom once Marie and I came in from the backyard, mascara smeared across both cheeks. She was silent and reserved for the rest of the afternoon

Glenn and Lisa said they needed to leave early to eat dinner and fall asleep in time for the first morning Mass. The leftover food was tossed out and the card table was folded back up and returned to Marie's closet, and once the party was over, Carla promptly returned to her car and drove back to Pennsylvania, as if our entire afternoon together had been a bad dream she wanted to shake off.

Meeting the family had been nice, but nothing felt different. An aura of concealment continued to linger. I never determined where it came from or why, but the Daly family played their cards tight to the chest. This behavior was likely inherited, embedded in my own genes.

Needing space to straighten up the house, Marie insisted that Neil take me out and show me around New

Brimfield. He agreed begrudgingly and led me outside to his Cadillac. When he turned the ignition, an Earth, Wind and Fire cassette tape blared from the dashboard speakers. He lowered the volume and backed out of Marie's driveway. We tumbled down the dirt road back toward the center of New Brimfield.

Uncle Neil sat quietly and offered no clues as to where we were headed. The man was still a mystery. My hope was that he'd start organically telling me more about Dad as our evening unfolded. The two brothers shared a slight physical resemblance, but Uncle Neil had at least fifty pounds on Dad. Based on my observations, they did not share any real interests that I could tap into, except for enjoyment of the occasional cocktail. Clearly their lives had diverged once my father left town.

The sun dropped over the hill as we drove and a radiant golden light settled upon us through the windshield. Neil commented about how it would be pitch black soon. He said we should probably stop somewhere because once it was dark the fifty-cent tour was over. He took a left from Main Street onto Cherry Lane, and drove past two flashing yellow lights. I watched the row of streetlights flicker on. He slowed down and parked in a gravel lot next to New Brimfield's historic Eagle Inn. The two-story blue building declared, *Good Food, Sturdy Drink*, on a sign with real flames rising from an iron torch.

Neil and I didn't enter the front door, which was the guest entrance for a small bed-and-breakfast, but descended a stone staircase into a tavern at the basement level. Inside was a collection of round tables strategically placed across a homemade hardwood floor. Wooden pitchforks, antiquated yokes, and old pulleys decorated the cream-colored walls beside a great stone fireplace. The bar was empty. An old man, tall and skinny with white stubble, waited anxiously for his after-dinner crowd to arrive.

"Steve," nodded Uncle Neil, pulling out a stool and plopping himself on top.

"Evening, Neil," Steve replied.

"Where is everyone tonight?"

"Not here, apparently. Bunch of regulars defected to that new sports bar on Route 10. Leagues are all that keeps us floating. What'll you have?"

"Maker's Mark."

Steve looked to me and waited for my order.

"Go ahead, tell the man what you want," said Neil.

"I, um . . ." I stumbled over my words because I'd never ordered a drink before. I was only fifteen, for God's sake, but maybe I looked older? Steve hadn't even asked to see any identification. My only previous experience drinking had been at that damn party of Rick's, which had cheap keg beer and mystery bottles of liquor. I was clueless about brand names and mixed drinks. Although I'd spent a significant amount of time in restaurants and bars—where Mom and Dad had worked over the years—I'd only ever ordered sodas and juice. There was an art to ordering a drink at the bar. I'd seen it in countless movies and television shows, but at that moment I didn't know where to begin.

Steve's eyebrows lifted. We were his only customers, but he was growing impatient with me. "Listen, kid, you ordering or not?"

His sharp voice pulled me back into the moment. I was on edge. After the last two days I was absolutely drained, my head heavy, my thoughts spinning. On top of that I was in a bar with my estranged uncle, being asked what I wanted to drink, when I knew it was wrong. I peered over at Neil, who smirked at me.

"I'll have a beer, please," I said.

"Okay . . . a beer . . . What kind? I've got about twelve on tap and twenty-five different bottles."

"Steve," said Neil, interjecting himself, "my nephew will have a Budweiser."

"Your nephew, huh?" Steve said, retrieving a brown bottle from underneath the bar and ripping off the cap with a flat opener. "A Daly family reunion." He laid out a fresh white napkin and dropped the bottle with a thud. He stared at me with purpose. "Whose son is he again?"

"My brother's."

"Thomas?"

"Yup, that's right."

"I'm sorry to hear what happened."

"We're all dying sooner or later," replied Neil, who shrugged and then winced over his first sip.

Steve turned to me and grinned. "I used to drink with your old man back in the day," he said. "At this very bar, in fact."

I nodded and took an obligatory sip of the beer, which tasted thicker than I had expected. At least it didn't turn my stomach. "Really?" I said, feigning interest.

"Sure. We started coming here about . . ." Steve paused and turned to Neil for verification. "What, was it right after you all moved up here from the city? '57 or '58? We were all about your age. The previous bartender, Forrest Jennings, fixed us up. Keep in mind the drinking age was eighteen back then."

"You used to drink here with my dad?" I said, starting to pay more attention.

"Sure, and your Uncle Neil too. Those were good times. Simpler times." Steve informed us that in honor of my father's passing he wasn't going to charge us for the first round, yet in an act of attrition he opened the cash register till and then slammed it shut. The machine bobbed and rang loudly.

I had never before given much consideration to Dad's drinking. Fathers all over the world drank and nothing about it was out of the ordinary. When I was old enough to notice, it had evolved into a private affair, something he did from the quiet seclusion of his bedroom, emerging occasionally for fresh ice or a shot of water. The rest of us simply developed a tolerance—out of sight, out of mind. We carried on with our own lives. But to think my father had started drinking at my age and in the very same bar where I now sat was troubling.

"You look like him, you know," Steve said. "I'm sorry that he's gone. I hadn't seen him in years but he was a good friend. I've got to unload some things in the back, but holler if you fellas need anything else."

"Sure thing, Steve, thanks," said Uncle Neil.

Steve vanished into a back room and the two of us were alone at the bar.

"Is this your first beer?"

I realized the first drink was a rite of passage in the Daly family. "Nope," I answered awkwardly. "I've been to a few parties before." Actually, I had been to exactly one party, but that was another story.

Uncle Neil chuckled to himself. For the first time I had his full attention.

To be exact, my first taste of any beer happened when I was seven or eight. I was home alone with Dad, who had pulled out a shiny silver can and smiled as he cracked it open. I heard it hiss as the gases inside escaped. As I recalled, it hadn't been his first drink of the day because the counter was already littered with crushed empties.

"Want to try?" he had asked, extending the can to me.

I shook my head no at first, only because I knew what Mom would say if she found out.

"Oh, come on," he had said. "It won't kill you. Trust me."

I really had no interest, but it was just the two of us in the kitchen and he had offered me the one thing in this world he valued most. I couldn't pass it up. And, really, it was empowering to do something bad. He waited eagerly for my answer, so I did what any good soldier would do and I bit the bullet. I grabbed the can from his hand, too wide for my little fingers, and took a long draught from it. I immediately coughed and felt light-headed as he ruffled my hair. He was proud of me and it was one of the few instances where I was proud to be his son.

Afterward, he smirked and leaned in close. "It's our little secret," he said. "Don't tell your mother."

I kept that secret all these years, so long, in fact, that I'd nearly forgotten it. There were many secrets I never leaked, intimate kinships I shared with both Mom and Dad. That's what secrets were, really: relationships of trust. Every time I kept a secret for someone, I grew closer to that person because I was in possession of information no one else knew. I had wanted to be closer to my father and if that meant drinking his beer or keeping his secrets, I was prepared to do that. Years later, when I found a bottle of cheap vodka stuffed in the empty space beneath a kitchen cabinet, I closed my eyes and pretended I never saw it. If Mom's frantic searches around the house came too close to his stores, I'd smuggle them outside and dump the liquor down a sewer drain. Loyalty was made of such actions.

I reached the halfway point of my beer before I spun on my stool to address Neil. "I lied to you all earlier about something," I said, lifting my hand above my cheek. "I told you I got my black eye from boxing."

"Oh? So you don't box?"

"Well, yes, I do box and I have sparred before. That's all true. But this black eye didn't come from that. We wear headgear and gloves. Pretty hard to get a black eye with all of that."

"I see." Neil crossed one leg over his knee. "So how'd you get it?"

"A girl."

As much as it made my stomach twist in guilt, I decided to share the story about what really happened with my so-called *friends*, the incident that had been ripping me apart for weeks. I hadn't spoken about it once. Speaking the truth was always difficult, and that's why I often preferred not doing it at all. I feared that lives had been derailed that night with Rick, no different than that day at the hospital when Catherine was terrified of Dad placing pennies on the train tracks. She knew back then about real consequences. Just thinking about that awful night made me feel sick. I lost Scott, my best friend, but really I had already lost him. Everyone had changed so much and there was nothing I could do to stop it. Who knows, maybe I had changed as well.

C HAPTER 16

AFTER BEING DEEMED ACCEPTABLE under Rick's high standards, and being pushed to say yes, I finally agreed to go to a keg party. By that time it was spring and nearly the end of my school year. The weather was temperate, more people spent time outside. Scott convinced Rick to pick me up that night because I had no other way to get there. On my way out I told Mom I'd be late seeing a movie. The living room was dark and she had the television on, and clearly she was about to fall asleep on the couch at any moment. By the time she woke up the next morning I'd be back in my room and sound asleep. Nothing would tip her off to my real whereabouts and I was safe to proceed.

I fumbled into Rick's car, a dark-colored two-door sedan with seats that folded down so I could sit in the backseat next to the alcohol stash. Scott rode shotgun. We drove so far into the country that the only light for miles was from Rick's headlights. His windows were down and the refreshing night air blew across my face. The nothingness continued for miles until we turned onto a dirt road and spotted an eerie orange glow in the distance. We ended up parking beside it—a gigantic bonfire raging in the middle of a clearing with dozens of shadowy figures surrounding the flames like pagan worshippers.

Tall pines formed a loose perimeter around the clearing. Beyond the trees was a luxurious log cabin with a deck, pool, and two smaller guesthouses on the property's edge. I couldn't tell who lived there, but that's the way these parties operated. Whoever actually owned the house was probably loaded. Hundreds of people, many of whom I recognized from school, were scattered across the grass, brandishing plastic cups, laughing, and absorbed in their own important conversations. Gigantic floodlights, which kept flickering on and off when someone accidentally sat on the power cord, pointed toward the crowd and across the clearing.

"Want a drink?" Rick asked.

"Do I want a drink?"

"Yes, did I stutter? Do you want one?"

"Yes, I do."

"That's my boy," said Rick.

Two metal kegs of cold beer floated among a mixture of ice and water inside an old bathtub. No one else was pouring drinks so Rick stepped up to the tap, grabbed three red cups from a plastic bag, filled them, and started passing them to each of us. He pushed the ends of his cup together like folding a slice of pizza and took a large swig. Then he informed us that a girl was waiting on him, so he walked off. Scott tagged along and soon I found myself alone, leaning against the wooden deck.

Quite some time passed and I grew annoyed, not wanting to stand around with a bunch of strangers. I wasn't the type to strike up a conversation. Instead I pretended to be absorbed in my own thoughts, but I frantically scanned the crowd to see if I was being judged for not engaging. The party seemed tame, though it was early. A lot of open flirting to set the groundwork for a later hook-up, and one guy in his underwear chased three sophomore girls, also not wearing much, from the pool to one of the guesthouses. They screamed in laughter as their gorgeous figures jiggled in all the right places. For me there was absolutely nothing to do but drink, and finally, after my third or fourth beer, I saw Scott approaching from across the clearing. He took long, lanky strides through the crowd and waved at me.

"Where've you been?" he asked.

"Right here," I answered. "You two just left me."

"Sorry, you know how it is, you start mingling and seeing all of these different people."

"Sure. Whatever. I just feel like crap tonight. Not really sure why," I said, although to be honest I knew damn well why. "Are we staying long?"

Scott laughed. "You're fine. You just need another drink. I would've been back over here earlier but Rick got talking to these girls."

"Oh yeah?" I said, framing my words in a way that made me sound interested, which I wasn't.

"I'm kind of like Rick's wingman, until he gives me 'the sign' to leave."

"Sign? What sign?"

"Okay, maybe not a sign exactly," Scott said, laughing nervously. "More like he punches me in the arm, but not too hard."

"Fabulous. So where is he? You both ready to go?"

"Not yet. I just left him. He's taking a girl into the guesthouse first." Scott's face suddenly went pale, as if he had remembered something horrible. "Ian . . . he's in there with that redhead you know. The fire crotch."

"Eveline?"

"Yes, the new girl. But you don't care, right? You aren't into her, right?"

I didn't react at first. The image of Rick and Eveline together in the guesthouse consumed my thoughts. I rubbed my red, itchy eyes. Everything unfolded in my imagination, all of the disgusting, sordid details. She didn't seem like the kind of girl who would even shake hands with Rick, let alone climb into bed with him, but now I knew never to assume anything about anybody. For years I thought I'd known my father, and look where that got me. Scott kept blathering about Rick and I ignored him. The party spun around me. I didn't feel well.

"What the hell are you talking about?" I snapped at him.

"I don't think Rick knew that you two hooked up," he said, attempting to defend his buddy.

"I didn't hook up with her, you *asshole*!" I screamed at Scott. "Which house are they in? Tell me!"

Shocked at my outburst, Scott pointed ambivalently toward one of the guesthouses, a cozy cabin near the trees. I marched across the moist grass, my heart racing and my muscles tense. I wasn't about to start a war with Rick; I just wanted to provide Eveline with an escape strategy, if that's in fact what she wanted. As far as I knew, she may have welcomed his advances. A concern for her general well-being drove me to the cabin, but in reality a hint of jealousy as well.

I pictured her incoherent, incapable of deflecting his nasty advances, and dragged onto a scratchy bed. He'd use her callously like one of the tube socks he bragged about jerking off into. I hid against the south wall of the guesthouse and watched the front porch, waiting for Rick to emerge for a piss in the bushes or to refill his cup at the keg, both very important considerations for a guy like him. And sure enough, a moment later he staggered out the front door, making a quick dash to the pines. He seemed to vanish for a bit within the trees. I assumed he was urinating. I had plenty of time to find Eveline before he took it any further. She could run away with me or slam the door in my face; it wouldn't matter to me either way. At least my conscience would be clear.

I crept through the front door and stubbed my shin against the end of a coffee table. The interior was unlit, too dark to see clearly.

"Eveline," I whispered, my arms stretched in front of me, feeling my way through the darkness. "Eveline, are you here?"

The floodlights outside flashed sporadically, affording me brief glimpses of the interior. Wooden beams ran across the ceiling, checkered curtains hung over the tall windows, a couch with large pillows was pushed against the far wall, and wooden furniture fit meticulously around the room. I stepped through an open doorway as the floodlights flickered on and off, and my eyes struggled to readjust to the darkness. As far as I knew I was entering a spare room or storage closet. Or, worse yet, a bathroom and I'd step into the toilet.

"Eveline?" I whispered again.

I carefully shuffled my feet across the room and ran into a large plush object, which I determined was a mattress, and I reached down. A small figure slept in the bed, and whoever it was had silky skin. She was either completely naked or I had touched an uncovered part of her body. I stood motionless for a moment and considered the possibility that she was, in fact, naked.

She didn't react to my touch. I felt her petite mid-section expanding and contracting as air was pulled into her lungs. *She's alive.* Once I knew she was breathing, I rested my palm on her bare stomach, the point right before it jutted out to her waist. I wondered if she had alcohol poisoning. Her stomach moved my hand up and down as she took deep, labored breaths. I'd be lying if I said I didn't think about doing *something*—if only for a split-second—taking certain liberties because we were alone and nobody would know. But that wasn't me, that was Rick. If I was sure about one thing in my life, I was sure about that. I shook my head and slapped my own cheek, returning to my senses, and commanded myself to finish what I needed to do.

"Eveline, is that you?" I whispered into her ear.

She smelled fantastic, whoever she was, like coconut hair conditioner. I grabbed what I thought was her arm and shook it gently.

"Wake up. It's Ian. Wake up. Do you need anything? Do you need to go home?"

She groaned, turned onto her stomach, and stretched out.

"No, no, stay awake. You need to answer me," I said.

This time I lifted her head off the mattress, dead weight in my hands and flopping side-to-side like a puppet. She groaned again and flailed her arms in a feeble attempt to get rid of me. I remember wondering how such a petite girl could've had so much to drink. And then it occurred to me that Rick might've slipped her something. He could be very persuasive when he wanted, and if that didn't work he was an intimidator. I wouldn't put it past him to spike a drink.

Her head was unexpectedly heavy and my arms started to feel tired holding it up. I leaned it against the front of my stomach for a break, and proceeded to try to shake her body to consciousness. "Wake up, wake up, wake up."

Her reflexes no longer worked. If she had been in a doctor's office, her knee wouldn't even have budged after getting hit with that rubber mallet. I considered the possibility that I'd have to carry her outside and make a discreet exit. She seemed to be fading out of consciousness again. She probably needed to have her stomach pumped. As I propped her up, considering my options, the lights suddenly flashed on and I turned my head to discover Rick Sharp standing in the doorway.

"Daly? What the fuck!"

I glanced down and saw Eveline. Her shirt and pants had been taken off and tossed across the room. I looked up at Rick and responded with incoherent babble, shrugging as I tried to think of a way to explain what I was doing. Seeing me with the unconscious girl he was about to screw, her head over *my* groin, must've been a shock to Rick. He probably thought I was trying to get my rocks off on her first, on *his claimed property*. I released Eveline's head and her face planted into the mattress with a thud. I made a mental note to apologize to her later for my inconsiderate treatment of her comatose body.

"Get the fuck out of here!" Rick screamed. The muscles in his shoulder and neck were twitching. I stood in shock, my body frozen and my mouth agape.

Every Sunday evening as a boy I'd watched *American Wildlife* on public access television. The show followed a wildlife expert as he traveled the world identifying unique species and teaching viewers about animal behavior. I often watched the show on a twelve-inch black-and-white television Dad had perched atop the refrigerator in the kitchen. Dad would be preparing dinner, adding ingredients and seasonings, and I'd watch quietly from the kitchen table. These were some of my warmest memories of him. With everything that had happened, I still had those memories. They were few, but they were real.

Every week the show featured animals in conflict over food, mating opportunities, or territory, and the expert always tied their behavior to a theory he called the "fight-or-flight response." He liked to mention that the response also existed in humans. In the end we were all animals, especially as teenagers. We fought over girls and we sure as hell fought over territory, which was measured by social status. These conflicts would continue throughout the course of our lives in different ways and there was no avoiding them. I had always been one to choose the flight response, running from uncomfortable or uncertain situations and surviving to be shamed another day. But for some inexplicable reason, I didn't run that night.

"No!" I shouted back at Rick. "Fuck you!"

"What did you say to me, *you faggot*?"

"Her friends are looking for her, Rick. They want to go home," I said. "I came to get her." I hadn't seen her friends, nor did I know who they were. And I certainly had no way of getting any of them home. Rick had been my ride.

"Don't try to grow a pair, Daly. Fuck off before you get hurt."

I wondered where he'd picked up his tough-guy lingo. Was it from his father?

"No," I said calmly. "I'm not leaving."

Rick suddenly leaped over a pillow on the ground between us and charged me. He grabbed me. The next thing I knew we were grappling and spinning across the bedroom. I didn't know what to do next, so I held onto his shirt tightly as he tried to turn me around for a head-lock. We ended up in the cabin's living room. I heard the smashing of glass as we pushed and pulled each other across the space. He shoved me against a table and a skinny lamp shattered to the ground. We rolled over the coffee table and a wooden bowl of pine cones and pot-pourri launched into the air. Small decorative baskets full of magazines and firewood were overturned and spilled out across the floor. Obscenities and grunts escaped our mouths as we attempted to overpower each other. He was stronger; that much was for sure.

Everything grew dark suddenly. I took a deep breath of fresh air, realizing we had made our way outside onto the grass. A crowd surrounded us and started cheering, as if they had front-row seats at a prizefight, and my muscles began to cramp. I didn't know how much longer I could hold him off.

Rick was tired of grappling and he wanted a quick finish. I noticed when he raised his right arm as if to throw a baseball, except his intention was to wind up for a knockout blow. With the crowd watching, there was no way he'd settle for anything less than putting me down. He had a reputation to uphold, after all. I was hyperfo-cused on what Rick was doing and I felt absolutely no fear. My body was prepared, the job of pure survival being a mindless one. Obviously Rick had no idea how to throw a proper punch, and he telegraphed his right hand as though swinging an axe.

His punch came slowly and I was no longer facing Rick in that dark clearing. I saw myself in the ring, sparring with Enzo. We were drilling counterpunches, like we did every week for hours. Bud was there. They said I showed promise. *That I mattered.* Inches before Rick's strike was about to connect with my face, I slipped to the right. His fist glided past and I fired my own stiff jab into his nose, sitting on the punch like Bud demanded at every session. The jab landed hard, and then I twisted from my right side to finish the one-two combination. I had done it a thousand times at the gym so my body took over. Whatever power was lacking in my quick little jab was avenged by my right cross to Rick's jaw, accompanied by a loud crack of bone. Rick fell backward and his head bounced on the grass. He was out cold.

I wouldn't remind myself to apologize to *him* the next day.

CHAPTER 17

AFTERWARD MY STOMACH WAS TWISTED in knots. I was anxious about my blatant loss of self-control and I felt guilty about the possibility that I had seriously hurt Rick. The guy was a jackass, but who was I to do what I did? So many emotions boiled up at the same time, as if awakening from years of dormancy. My only thought was how I had screwed up *everything*. Our altercation replayed over and over again in my head like a damaged videocassette. I'd have to say farewell to Scott forever, and Rick would undoubtedly take brutal revenge as soon as he had the chance. He'd beat me to a bloody pulp when I'd least expect it to teach me a lesson and prove to everyone at school he was still top dog.

I took deep breaths and held them in to help soothe my unquiet mind and strung-out body, and focused whatever faculties remained to piece together what happened after I'd escaped. Once Rick fell down, a group of guys crouched beside him to help. I didn't wait for any of them to attack me or demand that I wait around for the police. Instead I sprinted across the clearing, forcing my way through the tall pine trees with razor-sharp needles and onto the road. I worried for Eveline's safety. I didn't know what became of Scott and I didn't care.

I jogged through the darkness, peering over my shoulder to ensure I wasn't being followed. Headlights came from the direction of Wellbourne and I began waving my arms. An old red pickup truck pulled over and it was hard for me to see the driver's face until I approached the door. I recognized the guy behind the wheel, but couldn't recall his name. He had graduated from Wellbourne High School the previous year and now worked at the grocery store, but he was tragically incapable of moving on to the next stage of his life, still carting himself out to all of the high school parties every weekend. Rolling down his window, he asked me whether the party was any good. I lied to him and said it sucked and asked if he could spare me a ride home. He was tired from a double shift at work anyway and eager not to miss the upcoming West Coast football game, so he didn't require much convincing.

As we drove back to town I checked the rear mirror, expecting headlights from a pursuing vehicle seeking retribution for Rick, but none came. The night grew damp. Wispy clouds glowed in the moonlight and stretched above sprawling fields. Stars occasionally peeked out in patches and reminded me of catching fireflies as a boy with Mom's family in Fairfield Valley. We used to see hundreds of them floating through the fields and caught a few in glass jars. But with every passing summer we saw less of them, and these days I couldn't recall the last time I had seen one. Now they were simply memories.

I tried to explain to Uncle Neil and Steve the bartender, my captive audience, that all I could do after that night was wait for the consequences. *Police at my door. Letters from his family lawyer. Suspension from school. A sur-*

prise beating. These were all fair game and the clock was ticking, but nothing ever happened.

I don't know if he was embarrassed that I bested him, or if he didn't want any authorities asking questions about him and Eveline, but in the end Rick let it all go. What bothered me most was that I didn't know what happened to Eveline. I wanted to believe a kind soul at the party had looked after her and taken her home safely, but there was no way of knowing for sure. I didn't see her around school after that night. Soon her teachers stopped calling out her name during roll call. She was gone.

"So he never got you back?" asked Steve.

No new customers had entered the bar during my story, and to the detriment of his side work, Steve lingered to hear every word. He was completely spellbound. I couldn't imagine his regulars told very interesting stories day after day, or maybe Steve had just heard them all.

Uncle Neil slid a finger across the rim of his glass. "That kid sounds like a real son of a bitch," he said. "I'm glad you popped him one."

"He is," I said. "But no, he never came back for me and now he's gone too."

"Gone?"

"Boarding school in Vermont."

A few weeks after our fight, Rick and Scott were involved in a serious car accident. On the way to another party, Rick drove the two of them straight into a ditch—a giant crater in the ground. Rick's father happened to be working that night and was the first officer on the scene. He discovered the two barely conscious in the front seat.

Empty beer cans fell from the vehicle when he opened the door. He carried Rick to the backseat of his squad car and then used his radio to call an ambulance for Scott. Then he left before the other officers showed up to file a report. That's how Scott told the story.

"Now wait a second, he just left your other friend in the car?" asked Steve.

"The ambulance arrived about fifteen minutes later, I guess," I said.

"How do you even know any of this, if you weren't there?" asked Uncle Neil.

"That's also part of the story," I said. "You see, I was the only one to visit Scott in the hospital; I had to make sure he was okay. He only had some scrapes and bruises, and the blood vessels in one eye had popped. That was pretty gnarly."

"Wow," Steve responded, shaking his head. "Kids these days. We get it you don't respect nothing or nobody, but back in my day we looked out for our friends."

I nodded.

Rick's privileged life finally made sense to me. He took unnecessary risks and lived like shit never caught up with him—because it didn't. He had his own Get Out of Jail Free Card. Scott and I would've never received that sort of treatment. If my car—stocked full of beer cans—had crashed into a ditch, I'd have spent the following school year picking up garbage off the interstate, but not Rick. The world was full of two types of guys: those who broke the rules and those who paid for it. Guys like Rick coasted through life with no speed bumps or stop signs, while the rest of us clawed our way up from the bottom. Guys like Rick grew up to manage corporations or run for Congress. Scott and I would be lucky to earn minimum wage at a fast food restaurant.

Uncle Neil hunched to one side and dug into his back pocket. He pulled out some wadded money and counted out enough to settle our bill, minus the complimentary first round. "It's been swell, Steve-o, but I got to get the kid back to his aunt's house," he said, smoothing out the bills and setting them under his empty glass. "And keep the change, buy yourself something real nice."

Steve lifted the cash. "Oh boy, I'll try not to spend it all in one place."

Neil and I stood up and started walking back toward the door.

"Hey," called out Steve. I turned. "Sorry about your old man. He was a good friend . . . and always one hell of a good time."

I exhaled deeply and smirked at him. "Thanks."

Uncle Neil set his hand on my shoulder and led me out the front door. "See you later, ya two-bit bartender!" he shouted.

"Until next time, you cheap-ass."

Now when Uncle Neil started the Cadillac, he leaned over and turned the volume all the way down. I don't know if he needed to focus on driving after having a few, or if he was anticipating some kind of deep conversation developing between us. I hoped for the latter. The ride back to Marie's would be ten minutes at most, so even if we both grew uncomfortable we wouldn't have to wait long to escape. The beer I drank at the inn had certainly loosened my inhibitions.

"So . . . did the thing today turn out the way you thought?" I asked.

"What do you mean?"

"Funerals are big, right? People from all over turn up and pay their respects, the family spends all of this money on caskets and flowers."

"It was fine."

I waited for him to elaborate, but he said nothing. The inside of the car was stuffy.

"Oh, okay, good."

Uncle Neil stopped at a red light, ready to make a left turn. The mechanical ticking of the directional got my mind working.

"Good turnout?" I asked.

"I guess," he said. "Most of the people we invited came."

"Who didn't?"

The light turned green and Uncle Neil made a wide turn before correcting us back into the proper lane.

"One in particular. We knew when we invited her she wouldn't come, but she lives right in town, so we thought why the hell not?" He shrugged.

"Who?"

"Janice."

I waited a moment before I replied. There were so many new names and stories mentioned over the weekend that I had to stop and remember who she was. Janice was his second wife, the woman he left for Mom.

"She's still pissed about it all," Neil said.

"About what?"

"Your father, mostly."

We climbed the familiar dirt road toward Marie's house. When we arrived I noticed that all the lights were out except for a lamp in the living room window emitting a soft light. She had probably gone to bed and left it on for my return. The story of what happened with Rick was still fresh on my mind, and seeing that sole lamp in the window reminded me of when the guy in that red pickup truck dropped me off at home. I wasn't wearing a watch—I never do—but it must've been two or three in the morning.

The house had been dark, so I assumed Mom was asleep. Scaling our crooked porch had been easier drunk because my dizziness seemed to compensate for the warped floorboards. The doorknob turned easily, meaning I hadn't been locked out, but the rusty door hinges squeaked loudly. I moved as slowly as possible, pausing if it got too loud.

Walking through the house without setting off an orchestra of groans and creaks had also been challenging. I desperately needed a cold glass of water before bed because I was thirsty and hot, and I'd heard that consuming water after a night of drinking prevented a hangover. I reached for the cabinet above the sink that held clean glasses. A small lamp, sitting on a café-style table for two in what could only be described as our breakfast nook, suddenly switched on. The light was soft and weak, and I was startled by the piercing voice that accompanied it.

"Who the hell do you think you are?"

Mom sat upright at the table.

She had worn one of my old T-shirts to bed, her hair was tied up, and smoke from a lit cigarette curled above her head like a snake being charmed from the bottom of a wicker basket. I held onto the side of the counter to steady myself and played it off as best I could.

"Huh?"

"I said, who the hell do you think you are?"

Her volume had multiplied in the tight space of the kitchen. I didn't answer at first. And I didn't want to open my mouth because she might smell the alcohol on my breath; she used to brag about always being able to smell it on my father's breath, no matter the lengths he underwent to conceal it.

"It's two o'clock in the morning. Do you think you can pull this shit just because you live with your mother? Think I won't notice? Think again! So I ask again: who the hell do you think you are?"

She stood up and wedged herself into my personal space. I squinted to focus on her mouth as she spoke and everything slowed like a dream.

"Where have you been?"

I had to answer. "We just, we just lost track of time. We watched the movie and it got late. Sorry."

"You're sorry? Don't think I'm a fucking idiot!"

The veins on her temples bulged and her breathing grew deep and erratic. She was so angry I thought she was going to hit me across the face.

"Can we talk about this in the morning? I need sleep, I don't feel well."

I turned to leave but she put her arm across the doorway.

"No! You're a goddamn kid and you do what I say, unless you want to pack up your shit and move out. You're in *my* house. And that means you don't get to come and go as you please."

"I said I was sorry, *okay*? What the hell else do you want from me?"

She snorted bitingly. "You're just like your father!"

My heart beat so loudly I felt it throb in my ears. "Whatever. I'm out," I said, pushing past her outstretched arm like a subway turnstile.

I heard a loud thud from behind me, and when I turned, Mom was on the floor, vulnerable like a turtle on its back struggling to flip itself over.

"Mom! I'm sorry. I'm sorry. Are you okay?"

I helped her stand and she shoved me into the dining room wall.

"Don't fucking touch me!" she screamed. "I want you out of this house. By tomorrow morning, I want you out."

She stormed past me and up the steps, slamming her bedroom door. I remember standing for a moment in the stillness, hearing nothing but the ticking of a nearby clock. I grabbed a glass from the kitchen cabinet, filled it with cold water, and chugged it as I had planned, seeing my own disheveled reflection in the darkened window.

The next morning she greeted me in the kitchen as if nothing had happened. The start of a new day meant she had erased from her mind all of the ugliness from the night before, and the unfortunate event was never mentioned again.

Walking into Marie's house would be different, of course, and Marie wasn't my mother. I had been on my own all weekend, coming and going as I pleased, drinking with my new uncle, and there was nobody I needed to answer to. Was this how it felt to be independent and on one's own? If so, I couldn't wait.

Neil coasted into the muddy driveway and pushed up the gearshift. The Cadillac lurched into park.

"Looks like this is your stop," he said, suddenly realizing he wouldn't see me again before I left town. He held out his hand. I took it and we shook firmly. "Nice meeting you, Ian."

"Nice meeting you too." I opened his rather long and heavy passenger-side door and pushed it harder than normal to stay open, otherwise it would've closed on me. Then I turned to my uncle. "Neil, now that we all met, do you think we'll be like a real family now? Visit each other a couple of times a year for the holidays or whatever?"

He smacked his lips and looked out the windshield at the dark sky. "Nope, probably not."

I let go of the car door. "Well, like I said, it was nice to meet you."

SUNDAY

CHAPTER 18

NOT UNTIL THE NEXT MORNING when I opened my eyes on Marie's couch did it truly sink in that my weekend was coming to an end. Soon I'd be back to my regular life, yet I knew it would never be the same. My concern over the whereabouts of Eveline, and my uncertainty over Scott, would return to me like high tide. Scott and I had reconnected in the hospital after his accident, but it felt unnatural. Now I struggled to foresee how much longer we'd both keep trying to be friends, like a failed marriage where neither husband nor wife can accept the truth. The hardest part of growing up, I realized, was loss. No matter how perfect you thought it was, or how perfect you tried to force it to be, you eventually lost something. Not that loss was always a bad thing because it freed you up to make new memories, as long as you kept looking forward.

Marie was overly warm to me that morning, catering to my every whim, as if she felt sorry for me. She brewed a fresh pot of coffee and even fixed a batch of airy waffles, drenched in melted butter and drizzled with syrup. We spoke for a few minutes at her kitchen table as I ate, about nothing substantial. In those final hours we both detached emotionally from our intense weekend, acclimating ourselves to the real lives awaiting us on Monday morning. I showered after breakfast. Once again I cleaned my only outfit in the washer and channel-surfed in her vaudeville bathrobe as I waited. Marie insisted on driving me to the bus station on Main Street, but I told her I preferred to walk because I wanted the fresh air. I pointed out how I had already made the walk after Catherine left town and the weather was perfect. She conceded finally and gave me a strong hug.

As far as Marie knew I was catching the morning bus, but I wouldn't set foot on a bus until well after noon. The night before, after Neil had dropped me off, I pulled Marie's address book from a cabinet drawer and searched for Janice, the only person who refused to attend my father's funeral and Marie's gathering. I flipped through pages in a paranoid fury until I found it. I obsessed all night about not squandering my only opportunity to meet *everyone* from my father's previous life. I'd never be back again, so it was now or never.

I crossed a park in the center of town. A handful of crumbling benches were scattered around its rim, places where parents could watch their children play on the grass in the summertime. A marble statue dedicated to war veterans stood in one corner. Dozens of New Brimfield men had been lost in the Second World War, according to the monument, and not one of them was named Daly. I never expected my family to be on the statue, but I read the names nonetheless. An old man wearing a wool sweater, thick and fraying at the seams, sat reading a newspaper on one of the rusty benches. Behind him a woman struggled with a feisty Chihuahua and scooped up the dog's crap with a green bag she wore like a glove.

Wandering the streets of New Brimfield felt oddly like home. I recalled one of the afternoons I'd walked Eveline home, when all I wanted to do was dump her on the front porch so I could be alone again, and return to my weary house on West Street. Now I wondered where she had gone. I came up with a number of reasonable explanations: her father had transferred jobs; the family had upgraded to a house closer to Albany; or she'd caught a bad flu and checked into the hospital. Unfortunately, the rumor mill at school was in overdrive and I heard a range a stories, the most prevalent being her enrollment in an alternative school for pregnant girls. *That's where girls go when they sleep around a lot*, they said. As much as everyone in school manufactured ridiculous and improbable stories, no one really knew where she'd gone.

Eventually, I arrived at a quaint house down a cross street running south from the park. My head bounced like a dog tracking a bone, up and down, matching the address I had scribbled on a piece of paper versus the one printed on each mailbox. A brick sidewalk led to a front door painted deep red, offset by white siding, and I stood in place for a moment, contemplating whether it was worth continuing. What I planned on doing was completely unprecedented for me; I wasn't the bold type. I hated knocking on the doors of relatives I had known for years, let alone complete strangers who intentionally avoided me.

Three cars were parked in the driveway and it was a Sunday morning. I figured someone was home.

I bit the side of my lip. "Now what?" I whispered to myself, frozen in place.

I had a choice to make, and quickly, because soon

a nosy neighbor might phone the police to report a shady-looking teenager staring at people's houses. That was all I needed, to get picked up by the police. I studied the house and thought of new and creative ways to put off the inevitable. Shadows moved inside, beyond the curtained windows, and the anxiety I felt was a vise on my head, slowly twisting tighter and tighter. Our shop class used vises to hold hunks of wood as they were sanded into race cars that ran on carbon dioxide, but no one, as far as I knew, used vises on people. Not since the Middle Ages. I imagined my head was inside one, feeling the pressure on my skull until it would pop like a water balloon.

I'm tired.

I'm too tired to meet Janice. Not the right time.

I don't know how to talk to people. I act strangely.

I'll make a fool of myself.

Do I really need to meet her?

I floated over the concrete panels of the walkway and knocked on the bloodred door. It was too late to turn back now. I was surprised I had made it this far. My plan had forced me to trick my own mind into submission. Of everything I had ever done in my life, this was probably the most agonizing to date.

The door opened.

A tall, olive-skinned man answered. He looked Italian or Greek; thin, with salt-and-pepper hair, a turnip-shaped face, and rounded cheekbones like the smoothed ends of a car fender. His eyes were droopy and bloodshot.

"Can I help you?" he asked, his spindly fingers holding the door ajar. He coughed and the extra skin around his Adam's apple shook.

I stood, frozen, and said nothing. He waited for me to answer but lost his patience quickly.

"Listen, one of your little classmates came by here on Tuesday and I bought two boxes of cookies from him, so I won't be ordering more today. I'm sorry. Good luck on your little fundraiser, though." He started to shut the door.

"No, wait!" I shouted.

"Excuse me?" he snapped, reopening the door before it latched.

"I'm actually here to see Janice," I said.

"Janice?"

"Yes, is she here?"

"I'm her father. Larry Malone," he said. He eyed me up and down. "What's this all about?"

"I came to see her."

He turned toward the inside of the house, leaving the door open. "Janice!" he screamed.

"What?" I heard a woman reply from inside.

"You have a visitor!"

"A visitor? Who?"

"Yes," he answered, turning to me as he spoke. "A young man, named . . ."

"Ian."

"Ian!" he screamed into the house.

I heard footsteps thumping along, and a woman joined Mr. Malone at the front door. She stood eye level with me, her hair dark and curly, resembling the Mediterranean look of her father. Her face was more of an apple shape than a turnip, and like Carla, her hair was shiny and black. I realized that both of Dad's previous wives had dark hair, but not Mom. Is that why he had stayed with her for so long? I wagered that Dad's "type" was dark hair, but maybe after two failed relationships with brunettes he decided to go with a blonde like Mom.

The woman at the door flashed a half smile with teeth too white to be natural. "Yes? Do I know you?" she said. Her eyes were very dark. I couldn't discern the line between the iris and pupil so everything looked black.

"Janice, hi," I said. "You don't know me, but . . ." The veins in my head pumped thick plasma, throbbing, surging adrenaline, and I tapped my palm on my waist to relieve some tension. It seemed a numbing agent had been injected into my lips and I could barely speak. I was so terrified of coming off as a stammering fool that I wanted to shout and keep silent at the same time. "Well, like I said, you don't really know me, but you knew my father, Thomas. Thomas Daly. He died recently."

The smile melted down the sides of her face and she stared at me with those black eyes. Mr. Malone, holding the door open with his left shoulder, mouthed my father's name to her as if I hadn't noticed. *Thomas Daly.* A bad word apparently, one they never spoke aloud. Mr. Malone waited for Janice to slam the door in my face, but she didn't. She nodded at her father and waved me inside.

"Come in," she said coldly, briefly scanning the neighborhood to ensure I was alone.

Mr. Malone put his long fingers on my shoulder to steer me inside the house, in case I was some type of troublemaker. "Would you care for something cold to drink? A water or pop?" he asked.

"No thanks," I said, slightly aggravated because I didn't understand people who referred to soda as pop.

We traveled through the living room, where three

strangers sat on a caramel-colored leather couch. They stopped talking to examine me, as if I were a servant who'd stumbled into the wrong part of the house. The Malone house was plain and beige, not full of knick-knacks, pictures, or decorations like Mom had in our house. Ivory curtains swung from side to side in the front windows like flags of surrender. Janice and Mr. Malone led me down a narrow hallway to an empty study with two white French doors that he opened and directed me through. Mystery novels, the kind for sale at the airport, collected dust on wall-to-wall bookshelves. Empty spaces in the study were decorated with a sparse collection of family pictures. An uncomfortable silence hung in the air. The only sounds were a steady humming from a vent in the ceiling and the irritating *tick-tock* of an antique clock hanging over the French doors. The clock indicated to me that I could still catch the first bus of the morning, my "escape" bus.

Janice and her father directed me to sit on a leather love seat. Across the room was a small desk with an old fax machine and a round crystal paperweight. Janice took the desk chair, rolled it into the middle of the room, and sat on it backward, facing me.

"What are you doing here?" she asked.

I looked down, but not for long. My head was spinning, like a tire stuck in the mud, spinning but making no progress, and that's when I got hit with another fix of adrenaline. That precious hormone was the only reason I was still alert, but sooner or later it would wear off. For once I wished I had one of the liquor bottles from Rick's basement. That would've helped settle my nerves.

Janice repeated her question: "What are you doing here?"

"I . . . I . . ."

"Well, spit it out, answer me." She kept her voice down, but I could tell she was on the verge of a meltdown. I recognized the signs often enough in Mom. "If you're here wanting something from me, you can forget it, I have nothing. Thomas owed me thousands of dollars, but I've forgotten all about it, and him. I've moved on. I forgot about it all." Her eyes bugged out.

I exhaled loudly. "My sister Catherine and I didn't know about you until after he died."

"So?"

"I thought meeting you would be the right thing to do," I said.

"No need for it. You and your sister may've just learned about the *real* Thomas Daly, but I've known him my entire life. Aren't we all past the point of needing 'to do the right thing'? If you're feeling guilty, that's your own issue to work out."

"Why would I feel guilty? It wasn't my fault."

"Sure," she said, sighing. "I can respect what you're trying to do, I really can, but if you think I'm happy you stopped by unannounced, then you're wrong."

"I really don't know why I came today, to be honest."

She didn't care what I had to say, yet I needed to keep talking. I couldn't let her control the situation.

"I walked here, lied to people about it, and maybe hoped there'd be something at the end of it all, you know? *Something good?* Instead, I'm here and I figured out it's all for nothing. And you, you just sit there fuming over something that happened years ago." My eyes tingled and I couldn't swallow.

Something wet pooled on the bottom of my eyelids

and I fought the urge to blink so nothing would roll down my face. The last thing I wanted was for Janice to think I was crying when I wasn't. Crying changed nothing. For so long I had forgotten what it was like to cry. I always *held it together* and my heart had transformed into a thorny mass.

All I could do was keep talking until what I felt passed.

"I don't know what happened between you and my father and I'll probably never know," I said, wiping my eyes with my sleeve. "But why punish *me* for that?"

She nodded in agreement and pushed up her bottom lip. "I can't give you what you're looking for," she said, standing up and abruptly leaving the study.

I put my face in my hands and bent over, hearing Janice's guests conversing and laughing in the other room. They weren't talking about me in the study; rather, they were carrying on whatever conversations regular families have when they spend time together. I wondered if this was my cue to leave. I started collecting myself for a discreet exit when Janice returned with a young man I hadn't noticed upon my arrival trailing behind her.

He was much taller than I and resembled a younger version of Mr. Malone, except for his eyes, which were somehow familiar. Eyes the color of light passing through a bottle of amber whiskey. He was much paler than the rest of the family. I ran through all his characteristics in my mind and finally recognized what was so familiar about him: he had Dad's eyes. I didn't, but he did. Mom said I took more after her side of the family. She would've preferred I got nothing from him at all.

CHAPTER 19

RECALLING DAD'S FACE WAS CHALLENGING for me now, as if I were trying to remember someone I hadn't seen in years. Was my mind slowly erasing his image altogether? I couldn't say for sure whether this was a natural defense mechanism to help me deal with his death or if I was losing my mind entirely. I found it much easier remembering stories about him rather than nitty-gritty details. *Out of sight, out of mind.* Yet even as difficult as it had become to conjure him, I knew immediately when I saw the young man's eyes that he was my brother. Trying to describe the qualities of beauty is difficult, for instance, but most people say they know it when they see it.

Janice gestured to the young man, but maintained strict eye contact with me, as if she didn't want to let me out of her sight. "Ian, this is Cameron," she said, turning to him. "Cameron, meet one of your father's *other* children."

Cameron, who was a few years older than me, collapsed into the rolling chair vacated by Janice. She shot me a cautionary look and strode back into the living room to join her guests, quietly closing the French doors behind her. I realized that, from the Malone family's perspective, my sister and I were *the others*, and I suddenly felt guilty for thinking so negatively of them. I didn't want anyone to think badly of me. I figured Dad's family was crooks and con men trying to sell us a lie, but I no longer thought that once I learned the whole story. I couldn't blame the Malones for having such negative feelings about my father, and by extension, me. They probably hated me and we had never even said a word to each other.

My brother Cameron was very tall and I felt a tinge of jealousy. His build resembled a professional basketball player's, even taller and ganglier than Scott. He'd obviously inherited this genetic advantage from the Malone side. I shook his oversized hand and mine felt like a small child's in his. They were similar to his grandfather's claw-like appendages.

"So, you're Ian?"

"Yes. And you're Cameron?"

"Yes." He scratched the side of his head and tilted it from side to side as if to crack his neck. "I heard Thomas moved to Wellbourne and had two kids," he said, wasting no time. "After he left us."

The anger I had so easily detected in Janice wasn't present in Cameron; either that or he hid it better. Instead, Cameron had accepted the reality of what had happened and he seemed indifferent.

"That's right. Me and my sister Catherine were born there," I said. "And my—our—father passed away. Did your mother tell you that?"

"Yes."

I waited for him to say some words about our father, but none came forth.

"This is all really strange," I said. "We never knew about any of you until this weekend. I told your mother that, but I don't know if she believed me. It's probably why you never heard from us, but I wanted to meet you . . . as soon as I heard."

"I met *him* once," Cameron said.

"Dad?"

"Yes."

"What happened?"

Cameron was too tall for the office chair, which unlike his mother, he sat on conventionally. He leaned back and stretched his legs out for relief. I didn't offer him the love seat because it might've interrupted his train of thought. At first he had appeared unbothered by our discussion, though his face tightened as soon as I asked him to talk about Dad. He glanced away at the bookshelf and proceeded to crack his knuckles. Cameron had clearly run through the details in his mind numerous times.

"He came to town for his mother's funeral. Our grandmother. I was just a teenager back then and I wasn't even going to go to the service, but I decided I wanted to see him. My mother told me not to do it, that I would end up disappointed and angry, but I had to." He explored the room nervously as if he'd never seen it before.

"So what happened?" I asked.

"What do you mean?" He had grown confused, or maybe emotional, so I repeated myself.

"What happened the day you said you met him?"

Cameron smiled. I hadn't let him off the hook. "Do you really care?" he asked.

"Yes."

Cameron sighed deeply and continued: "Thomas—our father—stopped to check out this Corvette parked on the street, 5.7 liter, 350 cubic inch, LT1 V8. It was a black convertible. You know what I'm talking about?"

I knew nothing about cars. I only knew they had pedals and a wheel. And the gas tank, I knew how to fill the gas tank. "Oh yeah, that sounds badass," I said, faking it with a smile.

"Well, cars are sort of my thing. Are you into them?" The tension in Cameron's shoulders released for a moment as he discussed the Corvette.

"Me? Sure. Big time."

"Anyway, I stood next to him. We both stared at this car. He was smoking a cigarette and he looked over at me. I asked him if he liked the car. He said some bullshit about the world being full of two types of people: shit eaters and people who could afford Corvettes. Then he said that as long as we both lived, we'd never drive around in a car like that. And I said something about it being like a dream, and he turned to me and said, *It sure is*."

"Do you think he knew who you were?"

"I don't know if he knew or not. Probably. I would've known, if it was my son." His jaw suddenly clenched and the tendons on his skull flexed.

"Did you want to tell him who you were?"

Cameron didn't answer and shifted in the desk chair. "How did he die?" he asked.

"Cancer, I think."

"You *think*?"

"Well, he had cancer."

"So you have a sister too, right? Where is she?"

"She's back in Orlando, at college. My mom still lives in Wellbourne. I live with her."

He chuckled for a moment.

"What?" I asked.

"I was on the phone with your mom once too."

"Really?" I immediately wondered if Mom had known who he was and whether she had lied about it.

"Yeah, one night, when I was in high school, I got really drunk with a couple of my buddies and they dared me to call my *real father*. My mother never remarried after Thomas, but she dated when I was a teenager and my friends gave me a hard time about it. MILF shit. I didn't want them to think I was afraid, so I found your number in the phone book."

"And you actually called?"

"Yup. The phone rang forever and I didn't think anybody was going to answer and then some lady picked up and I asked for Thomas Daly. She said he wasn't home and asked if I wanted to leave a message. Being the drunk and smart-ass teenager I was, I screamed, *Yeah, tell him his fucking son called!* and I hung up. We all had a good laugh." He struggled to smile at his own story. "Hey, Ian, I'm sorry about that. I was just some dumb kid back then, like I told you."

"Oh, that's no problem." I wasn't lying, for once, because the phone call really didn't bother me. "I probably would've done the exact same thing."

I was so focused while speaking with Cameron that I didn't see or hear anything else. Sounds from the living room had dwindled and any distractions inside the study no longer registered, including the slow grinding of a ceiling fan above and a spindly branch from a tree outside tapping gently on the window. I hadn't even detected Janice slowly opening one of the French doors and stepping back inside. I wondered if she had been lingering by the door, hanging on our every word.

"Well, Ian, thanks for stopping by and I'm glad you and Cameron had a chance to catch up, but you should probably be going," she said. "We are with family right now and it's rude for us to spend all our time in here."

Cameron glanced at his mother, as if he intended to disagree, but restrained himself.

I stood up swiftly, like she had caught me doing something wrong—getting too comfortable with her son, I'm sure—and I tried answering but she cut me off.

"I'm sorry, that's all," she said harshly.

"No, no, that can't be all," I said, blood rushing to my face. "I came all this way."

They were treating me like a stranger, a sleazy door-to-door salesman. That's all I was to them.

"Listen to me, Ian," said Janice, her face twisting with authority. "I could've slammed the door in your face and told you to screw off, but instead I was kind enough to let you inside and meet Cameron. Now it's time for you to leave. And don't expect this to ever happen again."

"No!" I shouted.

Mr. Malone, hearing the commotion from the living room, stepped inside to investigate. "Is everything all right in here?" he asked.

"Yes, everything is fine. Ian was just leaving," replied Janice.

"No, I wasn't. There are a few more things I want to—"

"Fine!" she screamed, her voice high-pitched. "If that's the way you want it . . . Dad, call the police!"

Mr. Malone looked at his daughter questioningly. "Are you sure that's necessary?"

"Absolutely," she said, her eyes bulging. "Maybe it

would teach this little prick a lesson. It sure as hell didn't work for his father."

I was shocked, not only at how Janice was behaving and my own uninhibited response, but how the vision I had for this visit had begun crumbling. Never had I expected to be welcomed with open arms and declared an honorary member of the Malone family, but this sort of rage after so much time had passed was unexpected. We were engaged in a dangerous game of chicken, Janice and I. We waited to see which of us would back down first. I turned to Cameron, trying to gauge his expression, but his face was as expressionless as a mask.

Being trapped in an unavoidable conflict, a game of nerves, deciding who was the real chicken, reminded me momentarily of another night with Rick and Scott before the dreaded party. The way Rick drove, I was surprised he hadn't crashed his car earlier than he did. They had picked me up for a joyride after putting a dent into a cheap six-pack. We drove too fast over steep hills, defying gravity before crashing back down. Nature never made it easy to go against the grain. Rick swerved all over the road. He was far more concerned with turning the dials on his stereo than keeping us in the proper lane, but with a seemingly empty road it didn't matter. From the backseat I watched Rick steer with his knees as he cracked open a silver can of beer. He took a sip and foam spilled onto his pants.

He cursed and demanded that Scott grab the wheel as he attempted to clean up the mess. Scott nodded and held the wheel straight for him. Rick tried to brush the beer from his groin, blaming Scott for it all. He finally swatted

Scott's hand away from the wheel after chugging the beer, and threw the crushed can out the window. He struggled with pulling a second can from the plastic six-pack ring and the car veered to the left. Headlights suddenly crested over the hill in front of us. The speedometer flickered erratically between sixty and seventy.

Even now I couldn't explain my reaction to what happened. I didn't fuss or scream. Not a *Watch out! Stay in the goddamn lane!* I knew we'd all be dead in a matter of seconds from a head-on collision at high speed, but for some reason I didn't protest, as if fate were testing my resolve. Losing my life didn't play out as a major concern. *What life?* That's what I thought. I couldn't be the guy to crack, no matter what. I had to prove my fortitude. Somehow, crying out would've made me weak. I would've rather died first. Maybe that's what I truly wanted after all, but I couldn't say for sure.

Scott had been the one to finally crack, or at least notice the other car. He yelled, "Look out, man!" He pointed his finger as if he could've willed the car from our path. The other vehicle finally skidded to the left and sank into a ditch. The driver compensated and spun around in a full circle before launching back onto the road, tires screeching and horn blaring. Rick's car lurched from side to side. For a moment I suspected Rick had lost control, but the car stayed on the road. We heard a man's voice screaming from the other car. He didn't stop screaming as he passed us heading in the opposite direction, but his words grew fainter as we sped away. Red brake lights vanished into the darkness behind us and I realized that we had escaped. And my life was intact, at least what was left of it.

* * *

In the study, Mr. Malone recognized that the situation was spiraling out of control and he decided to intervene.

"Calm down, now, Janice," he said, turning to me. "Young man, maybe you should head out. I understand why you are here, and if I were in your position I would do the same thing, but as they say, you've squeezed all of the juice you can out of this."

"Fine," I hissed in Janice's direction. I stumbled from the study and stomped with long strides down the hallway. The dull conversations in the living room halted as I passed. Mr. Malone caught up with me at the front door.

"Wait, wait a minute," he demanded. "How did you say you got here again?"

"The bus," I said, panting as if I'd run miles.

"Let me give you a ride to the station. It's the least I can do."

Janice watched us from the hallway, leaning against one of the French doors. She eventually slammed the door. Cameron peeked out from behind the glass door, an apologetic expression on his face, but he said nothing. What could he say? We had just met, yet I was still the unknown. In the words of Marie, we could've passed one another in the aisle of a grocery store without recognizing each other. I didn't get the sense he was prepared to take sides against his family, the rest of which watched in fear, unclear why some strange boy had ruined their perfectly pleasant afternoon.

C HAPTER 20

JANICE'S OUTBURST REMINDED ME of my parents before we left Florida. They had started arguing more frequently and with a degree of rage I'd never seen before.
Sometimes there were disagreements about money, or
squabbles over who was going to do yardwork or house-
hold chores, but what family didn't disagree about those
things? I told myself it wasn't a big deal, that married
couples had disputes. Nothing ever got out of hand.

I understood now how their marriage problems led
to our manic departure from the Sunshine State. A few
days before my mom and I left, I heard them shouting at
each other through my bedroom wall, something about
Dad's job. He had lost it, again. Over the course of two
years in Florida he had lost four bartending jobs. I heard
Mom yelling about how Dad's manager had accused him
of stealing liquor. He vigorously denied it, but they fired
him anyway.

Mom stormed out of the house, slamming the front
door behind her. I heard her march across the gravel driveway toward our *piece-of-shit* car with no air-conditioning.
She started the engine and I remember feeling anxious
because it was raining outside and she wasn't in a good
frame of mind. I didn't want her to get in an accident. I

waited about five minutes for the air to resettle before inching out of my bedroom. Dad was alone in the dark, in his blue recliner facing the television. The glow of the screen shifted across his face like white flames.

"Where did Mom go?" I asked.

He didn't look up and growled from one side of his mouth, "How the hell should I know where your mother went?"

I spun around and went back inside my room, quietly closing the door behind me.

For most of the night I watched the rain dribble against my bedroom window and the palm trees swaying in the wind. Cars passed the house periodically and each time I expected it to be her, but they always kept driving by. The phone never rang and the house was dark once Dad fell asleep. I began to worry about her, but I also felt angry about how she could just disappear without thinking to call me, to reassure me that she was all right. I was too tired to stay awake, so I went to bed. Mom did come home, finally, the next morning. She explained how there was no problem; she had simply driven to the parking lot under the causeway for some fresh air and accidentally fell asleep in the front seat. I couldn't stay angry with her because the car made me sleepy too.

I glanced over at Dad, who was sitting at our kitchen table. He had lifted a fresh cigarette from the red crinkly pack on the kitchen table and placed it between his lips. I waited for him to say something. *I'm glad you're home. I'm glad you're safe.* Anything. Instead he produced an intense two-inch flame from a red plastic lighter, and dipped the end of the cigarette into it. He didn't speak or shift his eyes from the front page of the newspaper. After a long drag, he blew a thick cloud of smoke into the air.

Something had been wrong with them. I hadn't seen it back then. Or perhaps I had seen it, but I just wasn't ready to believe it. Dad had never been the traditional nine-to-five man, working at the same company for decades, like my friends' fathers, yet I'd never seen him so ineffectual. He withdrew into himself, defeated and despondent, and things only got worse. The way Dad avoided his problems reminded me of Cameron, who knew firsthand how much it stung to grow up without a father, yet refused to admit it to anyone. Cameron said nothing as his mother tossed me out of the house, but I could tell he wanted more. I don't know whether it would've resolved his pain, but it sure beat uncertainty. Dad had lived for years with painful secrets. He had tried burying them deep inside, but they eventually seeped out like a poison. I was worried that the same would one day happen to Cameron. And I vowed to never let it happen to me.

Now Janice's father was getting ready to drive me to the bus station. He snatched an old barn jacket and flat cap from a hook next to the front door. He lifted his keys from a homemade clay jar sitting on an end table, clearly made by a child's hand. I wondered if Cameron had made it when he was a boy. We climbed into a green Volvo parked in the driveway, closest to the road. He started the engine and pulled out. I watched toddlers playing in plastic castles on front lawns and giggling in swings tied to thick tree branches. I imagined it must've been a great place to grow up. Probably not perfect, though, because I finally understood that perfection only existed in fantasies.

Based on how my surprise visit had panned out, I

didn't expect any future relationship with Cameron. We'd likely never see or hear from one another again. Not that I desperately wanted to have another brother or sister in my life, but we did share the same blood and it seemed important we at least connect once. There were also Carla's children—Mark and Ashley—who lived close to their mother in Pennsylvania. I could try reaching out to them one day, but I'd probably send a letter or make a phone call first.

Riding in Mr. Malone's car, I sat quietly, theorizing over whether Cameron's childhood had been good or bad. Growing up with no father couldn't have been easy for him, yet having one at home came with no guarantees. Dad had slept two doors down from me. His body dwelled in our house, but I wasn't quite sure about his mind or soul. As far as I knew he may have considered leaving us when the opportunity presented itself, like he had the others. Or perhaps by that time he had grown too old and weary to start over someplace fresh, so he settled and was stuck with us. I wished I had told Cameron that being the person our father had settled for felt no better than if he'd never been in the picture at all.

I remembered how Dad always fell into a pit of despair during the holidays. Those days were devoted to solitary reading and drinking, but even the daily dose of convenience-store vodka couldn't lift his mood. Mom said he hated the holidays and they had always brought him down, though her explanation ended there. I couldn't quite understand how such a joyous season, one I so thoroughly enjoyed as a little boy, made him so miserable. But now I knew. Every Thanksgiving, or Christmas, or New Year, was a reminder of the horrible things he'd done, how he'd turned his back on them all. No amount of alcohol could remedy that crippling guilt.

Mr. Malone parked near the bus station on Main Street and let the car idle as we waited for my bus to arrive. Rather than drop me off and race back home to his family's Sunday guests, he decided to stick around until I boarded. Maybe he wanted to verify that I actually got on the bus, that I wasn't going to circle back and cause another commotion.

"I'm sorry about all of this," he finally said. "After all these years Janice still gets angry over Thomas. She was always such a stubborn girl, even as a baby."

I looked at Mr. Malone and nodded.

"She went through hell with your father," he said. As much as he tried to rationalize his daughter's behavior to me, he was also very careful about not being disrespectful. "I'm not saying your father was a bad man or anything."

"I know what you mean," I said, not feeling slighted in the least.

"The two of them went through so much, it would've been a miracle if the marriage had lasted. I'm sure you heard about little Tommy?"

"Yes, I did."

Mr. Malone lifted the cap from his head as if we were standing beside little Tommy's grave. "He was only a few weeks old. None of us could've imagined it. He just fell asleep one night and never woke up." His eyes glazed over. Before he bowed his head to put his cap back on, I observed the gut-wrenching pain he still felt over losing a grandson. When he glanced up, he hastily added, "I just wanted to make sure you knew, so you could understand Janice's side."

"Was that why my father left?"

"One of the reasons, probably. One of many. Your father had been married when he first met Janice." He paused. "None of us were very keen about that, but when matters of the heart are involved . . . well, you understand. Your father used to help Janice around the house while her first husband Frank was in Vietnam. He had been deployed for months, and a few weeks after he was killed in action, Janice found out she was pregnant. We all knew it couldn't have been Frank's."

I glanced at the clock on the Volvo's dashboard and realized that the bus was five minutes late.

"How did Tommy die exactly?"

He inhaled deeply and searched his memories. "Nature. You can't control nature. The doctors had a name for what happened, but I can't remember it. Having Tommy was an accident, really, and with Cameron, they were just trying to replace what they had lost. That's when your father left town." He took a deep breath. "Janice had also received this huge inheritance. All of it came from my wife's mother's side of the family. Thomas convinced her to sign it over to him and open a new restaurant. The problem was termites. The building he bought was infested with them and he didn't realize it until it was too late. They were weeks from opening and the city inspectors declared it condemned. Your dad didn't have enough left over to make the repairs."

I heard a loud mechanical grinding in the distance and suddenly the bus appeared, rolling to a stop beside Mr. Malone's Volvo.

"My ride's here," I said, opening the passenger door to climb out. I stopped and turned back. "By the way, thanks for the ride. And . . . sorry about all that at your house."

Mr. Malone smiled tightly. "Good luck," he said. "Now get on that damn bus before it leaves you behind and you're trapped here all night."

The bus door snapped shut behind me. I handed the driver my ticket and took a window seat in the fifth row. The bus was empty when it departed. I saw Mr. Malone circle the parking lot in his green Volvo. He stopped beside the bus. Our respective vehicles waited to turn onto Main Street. I looked down and Mr. Malone's eyes were focused straight ahead. I didn't expect him to look up at the bus window for one last wave, but if he had I would've nodded respectfully. I even visualized it in my mind. I could tell that Mr. Malone was the type of man who would only be concerned with what lay straight ahead of him.

Once the traffic cleared, we both made our turns and traveled in opposite directions.

I stepped off the bus in Wellbourne almost three hours later, in front of a swanky hair salon that had replaced an out-of-business greeting card store. The new business was all the rage for the local ladies. Mom even commented about how she wanted to put some money aside to afford one of the high-end cuts. At that moment, customers were coming and going at a steady rate. The door swung open and I caught a whiff of strong chemicals with an alcohol base. There were a few women inside having their hair trimmed and carefully shaped with sprays and oils. They didn't even notice me looking in.

From his seat the bus driver called down to ask if I

had any bags underneath and I told him that I had only planned for a day trip. He appeared confused and said goodbye, expressing an appreciation for choosing his company to satisfy my travel needs. Home wasn't far from the bus stop and I had nothing to carry, so I decided to walk. I wasn't in the mood to call Mom and convince her to pick me up when all I had to do was use my own legs. Sometimes it was easier to do things on my own.

There was an empty stillness to my old crooked house on West Street. I stepped onto the bowing front porch, the rotten wood cracking and grumbling with each step, and knocked casually, only after realizing the front door was locked tight. Mom pushed the curtain aside and glanced out the window, and was surprised to see me, as if she thought I had permanently left home.

"What are you doing here?" she asked. She was out of breath and undone.

"What are you talking about? I'm back from New Brimfield."

"You missed your sister. She came and went, as usual, typical Catherine," she said, and snorted. "You never told me when you were coming back and I had plans. Now everything is up in the air."

"Yes . . . I did."

"Oh Lord, Ian, I don't have time for this, but since you're back we can go to your cousin's wedding as planned. Your sister did tell you, right? She said she told you about it."

"Yes, she did."

"So, you're coming, right?"

The truth was, I had never felt so exhausted—both physically and mentally—in my entire life, but knowing

from experience how Mom would react to any change in
her carefully laid plans, I gave in. I could hold it together
one more night, that's what I told myself. Once we were
back home I'd spend the following week avoiding conversations, napping in class, and barricading myself in
my bedroom until I was recharged from my weekend—a
complete disconnection from my everyday life. Ironically,
the thought of this plan was all I needed to get motivated.

"I don't want to start an argument, you know, but I
really wish you had just taken the earlier bus home," said
Mom. "Being on time isn't important to you, I know, but
it's really put me in a difficult situation with this wedding."

"Fine."

Mom brushed messy strands of hair away from her
face. Even though it was past noon, she hadn't even got-
ten ready for the day. "Your cousin Robert is getting married at the Kent & Holbrook Hotel," she said.

"I don't remember him."

"Well, he's actually my cousin's son. You'll remember
him when you see him. You two met at that party off
Lake Saguaro when you were a kid."

"The Kent & Holbrook on Lake Saguaro? Must be
fancy."

"His family loves that lake. They couldn't imagine his
wedding anyplace else," she said.

The Kent & Holbrook Hotel was a luxury manor
overlooking the visually stunning Lake Saguaro, the type
of resort memorialized on postcards. Believe it or not,
segments of Mom's extended family had made smart in-
vestments in their formative years and were now comfortable enough to spend their summers on the lake. They
typically reserved a room at the Kent & Holbrook, went

boating on placid summer days, and dined on entrées with indecipherable names like borscht, kulebyaka, and foie gras. We'd visited the lake once when I was younger, but Mom cut our visit short when she said Dad developed a nasty "stomach bug." He spent an entire morning hunched over the toilet—having spent the night before at the hotel bar—and rather than get everyone else sick, we decided to go home early.

"You have to come with me," she now declared excitedly. "This is important!" She stood in place, lips pursed, waiting for me to say something.

Our ideas about "importance" were widely divergent. If attending the damn wedding was so important, why didn't she tell me about it before I left for New Brimfield?

"Well?" she repeated playfully. "Are you coming?"

I had been holding my breath without realizing it, and as I opened my mouth to answer a gust of pressurized air spewed out with my words. "Sure. Why not?"

"Oh, that's fantastic," she said, hugging me closely. "It's very important to me. Thank you."

For some reason the house felt more "lived-in," which was odd. Two mugs lingered on the dining room table next to an uncapped sugar bowl. Spoons sat nearby, stained with coffee, left to dry in sticky brown circles. Loose sugar grains had spilled from the bowl and scattered across the surface of the table, but no one had bothered to wipe them up with a damp rag. I scanned the rest of the house. From my vantage I also noticed a careless pile of long-sleeved shirts and blankets strewn across the living room floor, slithering between open to-go boxes and balled-up napkins. Tall brown beer bottles lined the edges of the coffee table. Some were half-full and had been used as ashtrays. I was puzzled. Mom had always kept the house obsessively tidy, yet from the looks of it she had hosted a party and didn't straighten up afterward. She couldn't have made this mess alone.

"Sorry about the mess," she said, as if reading my mind. She lifted the mugs and carried them to the kitchen sink, which was already overflowing with crusty pots and pans. Then she went back and tried to wipe down the surface of the table. "I didn't feel well this weekend."

"Doesn't bother me," I said.

I recalled memories of growing up with Mom's obsessive cleaning regimen and how this type of mess would've sent her into a rage lasting for weeks. People do change, that's what I told myself. She had relaxed her standards a bit, clearly, but in no way was the state of the house on West Street anything like the disaster of Dad's apartment after his death. Catherine and I had cleaned it out following a panicked request from the building superintendent. His studio was a different world from the one Mom and I had last seen, when he told me about his scheme to sail down the East Coast. A giant stack of newspapers covered the table next to his kitchen; cupboards were open; filthy dishes spilled out of the sink; clear bags of festering garbage with crawling maggots sat near the living room; and the dust was thick enough to write your name in. He had just given up.

Mom quietly returned to the kitchen and went about straightening up, as if my presence had reinvigorated her old self. I wondered if a significant burden had been lifted off her shoulders with regard to Dad, and whether, for the first time in her life, she was able to stop and take a breath. I climbed the narrow stairwell to my bedroom. My intention was to finally put on a different set of clothes, and mentally prepare for my cousin's wedding.

My closet was behind the bedroom door, which I had to close in order to access my belongings. The dark interior smelled like musty lumber and an abundance of dust always made me sneeze. I flipped through hangers searching for something presentable enough for a wedding at the Kent & Holbrook and nothing appeared. I couldn't recall the last time I'd owned a tie. Then I leaned into the closet and reached through a thin cobweb to push up a small panel at the top, my secret hiding spot. Lying in that dark space were three dirty magazines and a small baggy, which held a dried-out joint. I had hidden it for Scott months earlier, but he never stopped by to retrieve it.

As hard as I had tried to replicate it, my friendship with Scott before Florida was lost. We'd been hanging by a thread to begin with and the business with Rick effectively sliced it apart. Our lives had taken separate paths, which I supposed was natural. The truth was, I missed having him as my best friend. Now he simply existed as another lesson in loss. I certainly wasn't the same person either. What I'd learned about Dad and my family over this bizarre weekend had left an indelible mark. I crushed the joint and opened the window to send it into the wind like an offering to Scott's spirit. I didn't want the stuff, nor did I need it.

C HAPTER 21

OUR DRIVE TO THE KENT & HOLBROOK was through sinuous mountain roads. We seemed to circumnavigate all of Lake Saguaro before reaching a tiny hamlet on the opposite side. Stately lake houses overlooked the serene water like towers over a shimmering glass pane, ranging from the luxurious to weekend-warrior fishing cabins, each with a wooden dock of varying length. Mom hummed as she drove and messed with the visor to keep the blazing midday sun out of her eyes. She was in no rush and was relishing the scenery. Her window was rolled down a bit and she held a cigarette propped in the crack so her smoke blew outside. We had not said a word to each other.

"Everything go smoothly with your father?"

I was shocked to hear her ask so plainly about Dad's funeral, a topic she had avoided since I'd returned home. Her tone was so casual it seemed my weekend had been spent seeing a movie with him rather than witnessing his burial. She was probably still making up her mind as to whether or not he was really dead. If I'd told her he was alive and well, hiding in New Jersey, it wouldn't have come as a shock. I still expected him to show up one day and laugh about his death being staged, all a practical joke.

Given everything that had happened, I also wondered if Mom would ever be able to trust anyone again.

"Fine," I said, unclear of how to proceed. "I met his brother and sister, and some other members of the family. I stayed with his sister, my aunt Marie. Did you ever meet her?"

She laughed. "He never would've allowed that."

I scratched the side of my head. "What do you mean?"

"They weren't part of our life. Period."

Based on my years of experience discussing various topics with Mom, I decided to tread carefully. She was frequently apt to break down during seemingly innocuous discussions and lash out with grave threats about how if we kept it going we'd find her swinging from a rope or sticking her head in the oven.

"I also heard about the other women . . . the other wives," I said.

She lifted her arm to flick the last bit of cigarette outside. "I never knew about any of them when I married him," she said, checking the rearview mirror. "You need to know that. I only found out about them later, when one of their child-support letters came in the mail."

"So you knew part of the time?"

"Of course I knew, and so did your sister."

A firecracker exploded in my chest. My heart rate spiked and my vision became blurry. Betrayal was an emotion I had stomached well over the years, because it happened so frequently, or at least that's how it felt, yet now I couldn't handle it any longer and wanted to scream.

"Catherine knew? When?"

"I told her when she was sixteen."

"What about me? Why didn't you ever tell me? We're supposed to be a family but I'm left out of everything."

Mom grew defensive. "I was afraid, okay? Afraid of ruining your childhood."

"How would it ruin my childhood?"

"I didn't want you going through life knowing your father was a deadbeat who had two other wives and children scattered all over the damn state, and that's only counting the children we know about!" she shouted.

What she said was absurd. Everybody in Wellbourne knew all about Dad. Everybody in New Brimfield certainly knew. Nothing was off the table in a small town.

She continued, "When I was a little girl, my family was so close and loving. We had no real problems or worries—it was a different era. I have such cherished memories of them all. That's all I wanted for you and your sister."

"How did you just pretend the others didn't exist?"

"I did what I had to. I had to protect my children," she said. "Are you saying you would have *wanted* to know?" She smirked at her own question.

"I don't know." I was confused. She should've told me earlier, I firmly believed that, yet I also thought about myself ten years ago, five years ago, or even a year ago. I had changed so much and it was impossible to consider how the old me would've taken the news. There was a strong chance I would've grown angry, burying my feelings of disbelief and resentment until I became emotionally frozen, like my brother Cameron.

Thinking of all the possibilities—what might've been—was pointless now, because without Dad's death none of his past would've been exposed. I never would've met the Daly family or heard the contrasting sides of Dad's hidden life. In his own bizarre way, he'd made it all possible. And at least some good had emerged from our situation. I had met my family and now I knew. Knowledge, of course, comes at a cost. All of my confidence in the truth was gone, perhaps forever. Much of what I had believed over the years was a lie. Many aspects of our life had been arranged perfectly, in such a way as to make me believe in a manufactured reality. I had been so foolish. Thinking back, there had been so many signs, clues that for a less gullible person would've shown the man behind the curtain pulling the strings, but I either failed to notice or wasn't able to.

One specific memory came to mind, a day I'd never forget because it had terrified me so. Painful memories returned much clearer to me than the everyday mundane. Normally they're buried deep in the recesses of my mind, but once they surface they play out so sharply that I feel transported back in time. On this particular day, Dad had attempted to twist the truth to punish his unruly son, but visualizing it now demonstrated how reality didn't matter when you could spin a story to get what you wanted.

I had apparently been a terror in elementary school. *Everyone* despised me. I only had vague memories of those days. Everything I did was bad and wrong, and my parents had finally reached their boiling point. Dad drove me to the outskirts of Wellbourne on a tranquil afternoon when everything in the world seemed to fit together effortlessly like the pieces of a jigsaw puzzle. We rode in a red minivan that we leased, but a few months later would be repossessed for nonpayment. Leafy maples hung over the road. Clouds of dust lifted from the dirt road behind us and funneled through the air, a real whirlwind among the undisturbed landscape. Dad was furious behind the wheel, swerving and racing down hills so fast my stomach tightened. A child-sized pink suitcase, the only one I had, which had once belonged to my sister, bumped into my leg as the car jerked. Dad operated on pure rage that afternoon, yet there was a vindictive air about him, a slight gleam of satisfaction in his eyes that I'd finally get my due after all of these years.

He stopped in front of a small shack that greeted visitors to some kind of construction site. A man with an orange vest leaned out and waved at him.

"What can I do for you?"

Past the shack was a descending driveway and I saw trucks full of rocks, men in hard hats busily marching around the perimeter, and a light-brown metal structure that resembled a cabin.

"I'm just showing my son around," said Dad, pointing at me with his thumb from the driver's seat.

The man looked at him with a confused expression and glanced through the window at me sitting innocently in the backseat next to my pink suitcase. "Well, uh . . . all right, then. Let me know if you need anything," he said.

"Sure thing. Thanks."

Dad drove past the shack and looped past the main yard so I had a chance to look around. The men carried large, heavy tools. A network of narrow service roads went off in various directions like creeks branching out from a river. I couldn't see where they all went.

He stopped the car and turned around in his seat. "Do you like this place? Do you?" His face scrunched in frustration. "Answer me."

I didn't answer.

"This is a home for bad boys like you, and if you don't cut out the shit you're going to live here forever. Understand?"

I can't recall many instances when I cried, but I remember crying that day. In my defense, I was a little boy and children were expected to cry. I'd never make that mistake again as long as I lived.

"I don't want to live here!" I screamed, sobbing, barely able to breathe.

"The bad boys work all day and night. When they sleep, they go in there," Dad said, pointing to the metal cabin-like structure. "That means you'll stay there too. Starting today. Now get out." He reached over me and opened the van's sliding door with one hand. "Get out!"

"No, please, please . . . I don't want to go. I'll be good, I promise!" I yelled. "From now on I'll be good!" My miniature fingers—delicate and weak—clenched the suitcase handle so hard the blood ran out of my hands.

"I don't know. I just don't know. We've heard your lies and your bullshit before. How can we trust you?"

"Please!"

He sat thinking for a moment while I was inspired to try a different tack.

"What about Mommy? Doesn't she want me to stay?"

"Leave her out of this. Your mother is sick and tired. She told me to do whatever needs to be done to get you in line."

"Please, Dad, I'll do anything."

"Fine! Fine. Just shut up, will you?" he shouted at me. "This is your last chance. If you don't shape up, you'll be seeing this place again. Permanently."

Dad shifted into drive, cordially waved goodbye to the man in the cabin as we finished our sightseeing tour, and drove home.

I discovered years later that it wasn't a home for bad boys. Men who lie for a living, con artists or lawyers for instance, recommend that fabrications run as parallel to the truth as possible, because the challenge is keeping all of the details straight. Dad told so many lies over the years that he started to forget which was which, and that's when the cracks appeared. He brought me to that very same construction site when I was older, but it was empty and abandoned. That's when I realized it was just an old rock quarry. Our family was in particularly rough financial shape at that point. The mining company had relocated to Pennsylvania or somewhere else in the northeast, yet Dad pointed at the quarry and declared proudly that soon he'd be managing the entire operation, earning a big, impressive salary, and he wanted to show it off to me. I don't think he remembered our first trip there when I was a boy, nor did he address the conspicuously posted *Closed* and *No Trespassing* signs that lined the front gate.

When Mom and I finally arrived at the Kent & Holbrook Hotel, we coasted into the parking lot. The brick building was U-shaped, but the corners were in fact rigid angles that added an austerity to its massive opulence. A white porch wrapped around the front of the building, overlooking Lake Saguaro. Dozens of white-trimmed windows provided guests with an incredible view of the rolling hillsides and the lake's natural beauty. To me it felt cold and distant, the sort of place serving as the backdrop for an old black-and-white film. The hotel didn't suit my tastes, but it wasn't my wedding. I never had any intention of getting married.

We trekked across the parking lot to the main entrance. Under an awning supported by thick white columns were tall front doors, reminding me of a tour I once took in middle school of the White House. Mom and I climbed about half a dozen steps and entered the hotel like fake royalty. Green carpets with subtle imprints of leaves led to a mahogany front desk. The lobby was full of plush furniture, vinyl yellow flowers, and decorative bushes. A long table had been positioned beside the hotel's front desk displaying miniature cards with the names of guests and their respective table assignments. Mom rushed over to the table to snatch up our card.

"Where are we sitting?" I asked, trying to peek at the card.

"This is mine," she said, snapping it against her chest. "You have your own."

"Why?"

Mom and I had attended many weddings before where I was her plus-one and we *always* sat together. Dad had preferred to spend his days off in solitude, so whenever Mom was invited to attend a formal event of any kind, I was her date.

She paused before answering. "Because you're a grown man now. I thought it best if you had your own card."

Mom's response was bizarre, but I just shrugged it off. I searched the table and found my name card on the bottom left-hand corner of the table. Clearly the staff had added it at the last minute, written it by hand, and tossed it haphazardly into an open row. Unsure of whether I'd

be home from New Brimfield in time, Mom hadn't con-
firmed my attendance until the last possible second. Underneath my name was a designation informing the staff
I was without a guest, which irked me a bit.

"This doesn't make any sense," I said, flipping my
card over to ensure I hadn't missed anything on the back.
"Are we at least sitting at the same table? I don't know
anyone here."

Mom smiled. "Of course! Just relax, Ian."

I scowled and, under severe protest, jammed the card
in my pocket. I rarely followed seating arrangements anyway, so as soon as the event started I'd sit wherever I
pleased. They'd get over it. I did the same thing in high
school.

A member of the hotel staff in a black skirt, jacket,
and white blouse ushered loose guests into the main ballroom. Refreshments were being served, she said; a small
string ensemble played in the corner of the cavernous
room. I searched for anyone my own age, but found no
one. With the exception of a toddler who kept trying to
lift a finely polished silver butter knife, I was the youngest
guest, meaning my night would consist of sitting alone or
being asked awkward questions by the elderly.

Once in the main ballroom, the guests were funneled
toward a bar-on-wheels in a narrow anteroom, where
high tables were wrapped neatly in white linen and
spaced apart like stepping-stones across a pond. A line
of thirsty guests had already formed, taking advantage of
the free cocktail hour. Mom recognized a group of older
ladies, waved, and abandoned me to go say hello. I decided to wait in line for a soda because I needed a drink.
I didn't realize it at first but my mother's brother, Uncle

John, stood impatiently in line ahead of me. He turned with a big grin on his flushed face.

"Ian!" he shouted, gripping my shoulder. Uncle John was my height but with a round midsection. His full, reddened cheeks jiggled as he spoke. "You've grown up so much!"

"Thanks, Uncle John," I said, flinching a bit. I waited uncomfortably for him to mention Dad's death, but he made no allusion to it. I decided he likely didn't know.

He looked forward at the long line of people ahead of us. "The line for drinks is atrocious. They should have two bartenders."

"Yes, they should," I responded. The line seemed to be moving just fine, but I had only just arrived.

"What're you getting?" he asked me. He unscrewed the cap of a silver flask in his pocket and took a draught, and winced. "I just want a goddamn beer!" he shouted loudly, hoping the busy bartender would hear and speed things up. "It shouldn't take this long to get a damn drink during cocktail hour."

"You're right," I said.

He leaned in close to whisper something to me and gripped the back of my neck. "Want me to order for two?" he asked with a wink. His breath was hot.

"No, no thanks. I'm fine."

"Suit yourself."

Uncle John finally reached the bar and he made a point of being short with the female bartender, sighing loudly to express his disapproval with her service. I noticed she was young. She wasn't twenty-one, but legally it didn't matter. I knew girls in Wellbourne who waited tables and even though they were my age they were allowed to deliver alcohol to tables. Her dark-brown hair was tied up and she wore tight black pants with a white blouse. A pair of black-rimmed glasses perched on the bridge of her nose. She acted drowsy and disinterested in her job, which was probably the cause of the slow-moving line. She set a beer bottle down on the bar for Uncle John and was about to pour it gracefully into a chilled glass when he snatched the bottle, declaring it wasn't necessary. And then he wandered into the crowd to say hello to another relative.

I realized I was next in line. I ordered a soda. For a moment I was worried something embarrassing was stuck on my face, so I pretended to scratch it to remove any blemishes or bits of whatever hanging from my nose. Nothing came off in my hand, yet the tension mounted. The bartender's head was tilted as she worked, never fully looking at me. She grinned wickedly as I picked up my soda and nodded. As I stepped away, I sensed her tracking me with her eyes. There was something about her I couldn't quite put my finger on.

Back in the ballroom, I had to wave at and shake the hands of every relative I hadn't seen since I stopped wearing diapers. Not one of them mentioned Dad. Although I dreaded ever having to discuss him, I was slightly irritated no one knew. They all carried on benign small talk about the harshness of the previous winter or what route they'd taken to the hotel. I mentally checked out, smiling at the faces blending through the crowd while fantasizing about the cute bartender. I tingled with anticipation over seeing her again; very rarely was I the object of flirtation. She had probably turned on her charm in hopes of earning a bigger tip, but it was still exhilarating. I told myself

to forget it, but kept checking on her out of the corner of
my eye.

C HAPTER 22

I CONTINUED MAKING THE ROUNDS inside the grand ballroom, interacting with people I hadn't seen in years, some of whom I didn't even remember. Growing up I couldn't imagine a single day I wouldn't want them all around me—my family—yet as I stood at their tables, pretending to be interested in what they had to say, I realized we had reached an impasse. We'd given up on each other, like Scott and I had, and branched off in whatever natural direction our lives had taken. My high school English teacher Mrs. Garrett coined it best when she read a poem to us earlier in the year, one with an impactful line that I continued to mull over in my head—*nothing gold can stay.*

After my weekend in New Brimfield I found it increasingly difficult to even describe what constituted *family*, or at the very least what it meant to me. Was it blood, loyalty, convenience, obligation, or a shared interest in the trajectory of each other's lives? Nobody knew the first thing about my life—the real me—not friends nor family, and all because I was too busy trying to stop the cracks from forming in my fragile facade. If understanding one another was the defining characteristic of *family*, then no one came close. Stripping a person clean to the bone was the only way to truly understand their nature, and I suppose Bud and Enzo, or maybe even the other fighters who showed up at the boxing club from time to time, were the only ones to ever see me in such a pure state. They had witnessed me pushed to the physical and emotional extreme in the ring, a side of me without pretense. *Blood and sweat.* Not the version of myself I kept so regimented in public.

But even that group was falling apart because nothing gold did stay. I hadn't wanted to think about it, but the dreaded c-word had hit Bud as well. Cancer. Advanced stages. No one was safe from its clutches and its toll rippled across the community, affecting every person with whom it came into contact. Bud had announced it to Enzo and me one night after our training session. He said not to feel bad for him because he'd lived a tremendous life. Training generations of Wellbourne boys in the sweet science was all the fulfillment he needed. We were shocked and asked what could be done. He said not much. His admission was made before Dad's death, but like everything else I hated to consider, I'd simply pushed it out of my thoughts.

That excruciating night in the gym was the one and only time he ever mentioned it. I believe he considered the situation handled. We'd all continue training week after week, of course, as long as he was up to it physically, because the cancer had no power over him yet, or us. I visited his house once, unannounced, about a week after he'd shared the news. I walked through a shortcut in the forest from West Street, over shallow trails we had formed as children traipsing through the woods. Even after years of inactivity the wild hadn't reclaimed our ruts,

HERE LIES A FATHER

and that surprised me. Bud's house was ground level and designed in a manner that emphasized breadth. His vinyl siding was a dark evergreen and his shutters were a shade lighter than black. I opened his gold-framed screen door with authority and knocked.

I couldn't explain what had brought me to his house.

An older woman, soft spoken and wearing a knit sweater and tapered jeans, answered the front door. "Hello," she said. "May I help you?"

"Would I be able to speak with Bud? I mean, is he home?"

"Yes, he is," she answered. "Who should I say is asking?"

"Say Ian is here."

Instead of turning to one side and immediately calling out to him, which I had assumed she would do since I had requested him personally, she simply tilted her head and studied me closely to make the unavoidable connection I knew she'd make all along. They all did sooner or later.

"Ian Daly? Bud has talked about you many times." She smiled. "Your father is Thomas Daly, right?"

"Yes, he is." A familiar anxiety bubbled to the surface and I started considering ways I could steer the conversation away from Dad.

"I can see the resemblance," she said, opening the door wide. "Where is he these days?"

"Away," I said, nodding my head.

"Well, don't let me hold you up. Please, please, come in. Bud is inside."

She led me toward the living room where Bud was watching television, the sounds of a football game echoing down the hall as I approached. I crossed my fingers, hoping that he wouldn't try to discuss the nuances of the game with me. I didn't know teams, players, or any credible information to contribute to a man's conversation on athletics. He was so deeply focused on that game unfolding across a blurry box television—the dusty kind with hard plastic knobs—that he jerked up from his recliner when I entered, as if caught red-handed in a foul act.

"Ian, I didn't expect you here, what's going on?"

The woman who answered the door pointed to the couch abutting his recliner and said she would mix up a batch of frozen lemonade for us.

"Sorry to just pop in," I said, inspecting his dwelling like a dog sniffing a new environment. "I found your address in the phone book."

He chuckled. "That's all right, what can I do for you?"

There was too much about him I didn't know. I often imagined what his life must've been like beyond the ring. Students sometimes speculated about the personal lives of their teachers. They only ever saw them in one context, the classroom, and it was hard imagining them anywhere else. Now I had the same curiosity about Bud. I was getting a good look at his physical space and that was the first step in learning more about him. A shaggy dark-brown carpet, which emitted the stench of burned tobacco, spread across the room. The space was dark, except for a sliver of light coming in from an open patio window. His cream-colored walls held family portraits and wooden shelving with commemorative plates and wildlife figurines. A blue duck border, sitting level under the ceiling line, ran vertical across the top of the room.

He waited patiently for me to answer his initial question. *What's going on?*

"You know," I stuttered. "I'm sorry, I can't remember. There was something really important I had to ask and it's gone now. Has that ever happened to you?"

"Oh sure," he smiled. "Tons of times."

Bud nonchalantly reached over to the side of his recliner. I couldn't see what he was doing from the couch. I thought he was reaching for a cigarette, something Mom did for every conversation, but instead he pulled up a clear plastic mask. He fiddled a bit with something else out of my view and then began holding the mask up to his nose and mouth. He took deep, labored breaths, his chest swelling and cresting like waves on the beach, and I suddenly felt guilty that maybe my surprise visit had worked him up. He lifted the mask to speak.

"Doctor's orders," he said. "I need to take this oxygen whenever it gets hard to breathe."

He never brought the oxygen tank to the gym.

"Are you all right?" I asked. "I can come back another time."

"Fine, it's fine."

We both turned to the television and pretended to watch the game while Bud caught his breath.

The woman who'd answered the door, who I learned later was his wife Jill, suddenly danced into the room with two tall glasses of lemonade on ice. She handed a glass to each of us and set out adjusting the pillow propped behind Bud's shoulders. He gripped her arm and said it wasn't necessary, he wasn't comatose or anything. She shook him off and wandered back into the kitchen. Bud lowered the mask and took a sip of his drink.

"You hear about Enzo's match?"

"No. I haven't yet. I mean, I knew he was fighting in

Albany last week, but I didn't know how it turned out."

"First place," he said. "That kid's a prodigy."

"That's fantastic."

He took a quick sip. "Another first-place medal to throw in his pile."

"I'll have to ask him about it next time I see him."

Bud carefully laid his glass, half-empty, on the coffee table. "You know, Ian, we've been missing you at the gym for the last few weeks. Where have you been?"

I looked down at the shaggy carpet. "Sorry. I've been busy."

"With what?"

"Bunch of work at school and my mom has been needing me to do more things around the house. I need to help her because it's just the two of us right now, until my Dad finishes his job search."

"Been talking to Enzo at the gym," he said, biting one end of his lip. "He said you've been going to these parties. Drinking a bunch."

I could feel hot blood travel to my cheeks. "I only went to one."

"You know, if you want to stay in good shape you can't be doing that. That stuff will wreck you."

I nodded and exhaled loudly because I was embarrassed. After a few seconds I answered ambiguously without making eye contact: "I know."

One of the football teams on the television scored, but failed to get an extra point. Immediately after, the network went to a commercial break. The first advertisement was for a new sport utility vehicle that was so effective the driver was teleported across rough terrains to show its resiliency. In one scene he drove across the Arctic tundra and a pack of majestic wolves trotted alongside.

"There's an old story I've shared with some of the guys at the gym over the years, especially if I noticed they needed to hear it," Bud said, pausing to take a few drags of oxygen. "Back in the fifties I had this teacher, Mrs. Waxman, a scary lady who loved smacking our knuckles with a wooden ruler. One day she asked us to read this Indian myth about these two wolves. I know it sounds silly but the story really stuck with me all these years." He stopped for more of the invisible relief seeping from the clear plastic mask. He looked like he was worried about burning out his lungs in one sitting. "A grandfather told his son that these two wolves live in all of us, one good and one evil, and they are constantly battling for supremacy. At the end of the story the boy asks his grandfather, who is very old and wise, which of the wolves won inside him? The grandfather pauses to think for a moment and says solemnly: *The one I fed.*"

Bud had seen right through me, as everyone in Wellbourne had seen through Dad. All it ever took was someone running into my father at the liquor store, or driving our jalopy around town in one of his frenzied states, to connect the dots. Bud explained how he often shared the story of the two wolves with troubled fighters who turned up at the gym over the years, angry boys who grew up to be troubled men, addicts, criminals, or deadbeats, yet the occasional few took his story to heart and did better. The concept was simple.

Besides his oxygen mask and weakened state, he never acted like there was anything wrong with him. Personal dignity was important to him. He had obviously made peace with his fate, and didn't dwell on it. Bud was differ-

ent from my father in many ways, though one trait they
both shared was not being eager to talk about the end.

I laid my empty lemonade glass on the coffee table,
partially melted ice cubes piled at the bottom, and stood
up to say goodbye. Jill stuck her head out from the
kitchen and said it had been nice meeting me. Bud struggled up from his chair and gave me a serious handshake.
He didn't say a word, but I'd heard everything he said.
All that was left to do was keep the good wolf fed.

Bud would die about three months later. So many
cars would be parked at the funeral home for his wake
that some would say all of Wellbourne must've been in
attendance.

CHAPTER 23

I ALWAYS CONSIDERED MYSELF OUTGOING and extroverted, like Mom, but recently my feelings on the matter had shifted. It was what I wanted so badly to be, but the truth was, I hated large crowds and sustaining conversations. I sipped my soda, watered down from the melting ice, and watched Mom circulate the room like a movie star. She worked the crowd like the night was in her honor. I was in awe that she had so much energy to expend socializing, but my other self dripped with envy. I assured myself I did possess redeeming qualities. I simply had to discover what they were.

I approached the bar to the side of the grand ballroom for a refill and to see if I could get more attention from the cute bartender. My mystery girl was vigorously wiping down the surface of her workstation with a disinfectant rag, her dainty arms flexing with force. In a moment of frustration she blew a loose strand of brown hair from her face. I leaned my elbow against the bar to appear confident, but the entire structure jolted about an inch backward, thanks to a disengaged wheel brake.

"Oh, sorry," I said, cautiously placing my empty cup on the counter. "I just need a refill."

"No problem," she said, smiling and pushing the

bar-on-wheels back to its original spot by locating the divots they'd left on the plush carpet.

She refilled my cup with one of those bartending guns that shot eight different flavors of soda. We didn't say a word to each other and she playfully dropped a cherry into my soda once she'd filled it to the very top, although I hadn't asked for one.

"Thanks," I said with a smile, plucking the cherry out by its stem.

She smiled too and stuck her bartending gun back in its holster.

"Busy tonight?" I asked, casually sipping my refill. I dropped the cherry onto a white cocktail napkin and balled it up. When she turned to straighten a bottle I covertly tossed it into a nearby garbage can.

"Not now. It's slowed down," she said. "But I'm working the reception later. Are you going to be at that?"

"Yes, of course. My cousin is the one getting married."

"What's his name?"

"Umm, that's a good question," I said, smirking. "Okay, he's not actually my cousin. He's my mom's cousin's son, if that makes sense. I met him once years ago but I don't think either of us even remembers. My mom dragged me here."

She laughed. There was a memorable quality to it, like I had seen her on television before or heard her on the radio.

"What's so funny?" I asked.

"Gosh, Ian, that's the most honest thing I've ever heard you say."

My smile melted and for a brief moment I was terrified. How did she know my name? I checked my shirt to make sure I hadn't been fitted with one of those dumb temporary name tags and then I looked up at her in distress. "Do I know you?" I asked.

"Maybe," she said.

"Where are you from?" I thought knowing the name of her hometown would help jog my memory. As I waited for her response I could tell she enjoyed making me squirm.

"Wellbourne High School," she said, smiling, but this time apprehensively.

"What's your name again?"

"It's me, Ian." She looked down, "Eveline."

Eveline? Eveline Ryan?

The shock hit me as hard as the day Catherine called me about Dad. As excited as I felt to reconnect with her, I couldn't think of a damn thing to say.

"You dyed your hair."

"Oh, this?" she said, twirling a piece with her finger. "I needed a change."

"I liked your red hair." I searched the carpet's floral pattern—stalling—desperately scanning its leafy scrolls, following a labyrinthine design that I wished would take me away.

How had I not recognized her? She'd changed her hair, not her face. I should've seen it. Whenever I closed my eyes to picture Eveline, the only part of her I saw was that fiery mass of curly red hair, which was now gone. Her hair wasn't the only characteristic to throw me off. She carried herself differently. The girl behind the bar wasn't the same. Something inside her had been lost, perhaps extinguished. Her hair was now dark, dull, and straightened. The skin that had once reminded me of smooth marble appeared unwell. Besides a complete shift in appearance, I also convinced myself that I had never expected to see her again, let alone at my cousin's wedding, and that's why I'd failed to recognize her.

"Are you in school around here or something?" I asked. I was terrified our conversation would lead to that night, a topic very likely on both of our minds. I dreaded its expected arrival.

"No. Not yet," she murmured.

Mom suddenly called out to me from the ballroom, the first time in years I was actually thankful that she requested my presence. The guests had taken their seats and the chandelier lights dimmed. The ceremony was about to begin. I waved at Mom to acknowledge that I'd heard her. As if abruptly regaining consciousness, Eveline and I were thrust back into our neutral roles of guest and bartender. Neither of us wanted it to happen, but the formalities of the occasion got in the way of what we really wanted to say. There was simply no time to properly catch up before the ceremony.

"I better go. If I don't take my seat now I'll have to stand in the back," I said, realizing she had filled my cup back up to the brim. Not wanting to spill my drink on the carpet, I held it delicately in both hands like an active grenade. I was done making messes for her to clean up. I started heading back to the main ballroom when she called out to me.

"Ian, wait." She stepped out from behind the bar and took hold of my wrist. I looked down at my arm, under her complete control, and back up to her face. "I have to tell you something," she said.

Mom called out again, clearly irritated and confused

as to why I was more interested in talking to some random bartender than witnessing the start of her cousin's
son's wedding. I waved Mom away. For once she'd have
to be the one inconvenienced, because I needed to hear
what Eveline had to say.

"Yes?" I asked.

"I never got a chance to talk with you about that
night," she said.

"What night?" I don't know why I played dumb,
probably habit.

"The party."

Everything around me slowed as if in a dream. I
heard the din of wooden chairs scraping across the por-
table bamboo floor in the ballroom, which once cleared
would be opened for late-night dancing. The chairs were
lined up into neat rows. The guests grew quiet in anticipation, as if they were in a movie theater when the house
lights went out and the projector flickered on. I focused
on Eveline's face, waiting, simultaneously ignoring Mom
behind me. Without a doubt she was looking on at me
frantically. I could almost feel her aggravation over being
ignored fill the room like a noxious gas. The back of my
neck felt hot.

Eveline began to speak, but as if muted. I was too
busy stressing over Mom. I watched her lips move yet I
comprehended nothing. And then I heard her clearly.

". . . I know what *really* happened . . ."

"You do?" I replied.

I expected a hard slap across the face or a torrent of
curses, screams about how I had ruined her life. At that
moment I resembled someone with horrible abdominal
pain; I only knew that because I was reflected in the large

mirror hanging behind the bar. I didn't know what to say because I was too damn worried that she had known about the liberties I had considered taking with her exquisite body, lifeless in the guesthouse. In my defense, I had not succumbed to my urges, and eventually I had stopped Rick from going down an even darker road.

Before Eveline opened her mouth again, she leaned in close. I was ready for the pain. I deserved it.

"I wanted to say thanks," she said, kissing me on the cheek. "You're one of the good guys, Ian Daly."

My mouth hung open. She smiled at me again before turning around and sashaying back to the bar.

"You better get in there," she said over her shoulder.

I cleared my throat. "You're right."

I found Mom in the ballroom, impatient. She held in her dissatisfaction, but made it clear she was angry with me by bulging her eyes out. I felt dizzy, like I had actually said yes to Uncle John's smuggled booze, but really it was Eveline. In my wildest dreams I never thought we'd cross paths again and certainly not openly refer to that night, rather than sweeping it under the rug. Eveline was stronger than I thought, stronger than anyone at school gave her credit for. She'd left town after it happened, yes, but it seemed like she hadn't let that night define her. The girls at school had blamed her for what happened, I'd heard their talk. They called her a slut, a cock tease, and made up stories about her. One of the craziest had been that she was sent to a reform school for promiscuous and pregnant girls. I knew better than to believe their ridiculous lies. Those girls wanted to spin their own version of what happened for their own twisted amusement.

I took my place next to Mom in the ballroom. The

wedding ceremony was short and not particularly religious or traditional. I wasn't sure what to call the man
who conducted it, whether he was a priest, minister, or
pastor. I didn't really know the difference, anyway. The
"presiding man" wore a long white robe without any
symbols or decorations that would've tipped me off to
his religious affiliations. The bride and groom decided
they wanted it short and sweet, since it wasn't happening
in a church. They kissed and greeted the cheering crowd
as husband and wife, shuffling down a stairwell to take
pictures outside by the lake before sunset.

I couldn't deny that the bride and groom looked happy
together, and that the ceremony was beautiful, but all I
kept thinking about was how I'd never get married. I had
no visions or fantasies about my future. I would rather
live alone for the rest of my life like Uncle Neil than be
stuck with someone who either hated my guts or planned
to leave me for somebody else. I wasn't much of a catch
either. I was a substandard student with no real interests
or talents, floating through life without direction. My
guidance counselor, Mr. Kimball, a pear-shaped man with
halitosis, had scheduled me for a career assessment exam
on this outdated desktop computer and the results had
come back inconclusive. The guy was a real pain.

He was balding and enjoyed wearing bright ties with
yellow smiley faces. Months before the career assessment debacle, he called me into his office after one of my
teachers, he wouldn't say who, complained that all I did
was sleep in class. He asked me if everything was good at
home. I told him I lived with my mother and that I was
just having a hard time sleeping at night, to which he
responded that there was nothing in my file about a diag-

nosed sleeping disorder and that from now on I needed to work on staying awake in school. Then he tried to get slick and talk about what might've been "troubling" me.

A shrill alarm had sounded in my head, a skull-drilling tension, and a feeling of dread spread throughout my body. I wanted to stand up, make an excuse, and dart from his office as quickly as possible. I screamed at my own brain to shut up and just say whatever he wanted to hear until I could get away. And then I thought about rabbits. Rabbits literally scared themselves to death. Sometimes when these unassuming, fluffy little creatures sensed an impending attack from a deadly predator, they shook themselves into cardiac arrest. I imagined myself shaking violently in Kimball's office chair before my spine snapped like a twig and I spit thick patches of blood all over his desk. Instead, I picked up a Magic 8 Ball sitting on his desk, shook it, and informed him: "Everything is fantastic. Outlook is good."

The worst part about my meeting with Mr. Kimball was how he had called Mom afterward, which I never asked him to do. She was fixing up our house on West Street, wearing a ripped red T-shirt, when I came home. Her blond hair was covered in blotches of paint that had splattered as she'd rolled out the walls. She sat at the kitchen table with nothing in front of her but a large mug of cold black coffee, a pack of cigarettes, and a red plastic lighter. One of her legs was folded over the other and she sat at an angle, smoking with a concerned expression, gazing out of the kitchen window at the feeble attempts of a hopping bird.

"What's wrong?" I asked.

Her eyes had grown red and she dramatically slapped

her hand over her mouth, the cigarette dangling between her fingers. "I got a call today from your school," she said, exhibiting the signs of a person who was out of breath. "A Mr. Kimball?"

"Okay. What did he want?"

"He said you were called down to his office for sleeping too much in class, and that you two talked, and that he thinks you're depressed," she said, shifting from choked up to absolutely furious in seconds. "What the hell did you tell him?"

"Nothing, I swear. I didn't tell him anything, seriously!"

"Don't lie to me, you know I hate lying."

"Nothing, I said nothing. I just haven't been sleeping well lately and sometimes I get tired in school. It's not a big deal."

"Well, it must be a big deal, because this man is asking personal questions about our family. What did you say to him? Did he ask about your father?" She paused for a deep drag on her cigarette and then clenched her jaw. "I hope you feel better from your little talk, I really do."

I stood motionless like this random wooden column I remembered from an old house we lived in. This particular column had been decorative and hollow, non–load bearing, and built simply to run electrical wires from the attic to the ground floor. We all kept bumping into it by accident when we first moved in, but soon we got used to it, internalizing its inherent uselessness. In time the column was as good as invisible. No one gave it any further thought. Without realizing it, I started pulling at my lips with my forefinger and thumb, kneading the dry flaps between my own panicked breaths. I didn't know what to say or do next.

"I'm sorry," I finally said. "I didn't even ask to go to his office. I didn't mean for any of this to happen."

"You should be. Do you want everyone to know our business?"

"No."

"Well, then you've got to think for once in your life. Think about something other than yourself!"

"I'm sorry," I mumbled.

She finished her cigarette in record time and ground it against the bottom of a clear glass ashtray.

CHAPTER 24

ONCE THE CEREMONY WAS OVER the hotel staff emerged from the kitchen like worker bees to transform the room for the reception. They moved the tables in, covered them with linen, shiny silverware, fine china, and floral centerpieces made of pink roses and hydrangeas, spacing everything out equidistantly across the ballroom. The chairs we had used for the ceremony were moved from the straight rows and distributed evenly around the tables so everyone had a place to sit for dinner. The process took no time at all and the guests were too busy being chummy to notice the finer details. Everyone seemed to exist in a dreamy glow and I couldn't tell whether it was the alcohol taking effect or the atmosphere.

Mom stood beside me, clutching her place card. "Did you find your table yet?" she asked, scrutinizing empty gaps across the ballroom before fixating on one spot. "I'm at table five. There's someone I want you to see."

"Sure," I said, looking down at my card and feeling relieved, for the first time that day, that I was also assigned to table five.

Mom walked off with no warning, expecting me to follow. I trailed her through flocks of guests clogging the walkways as they laid blazers or shawls on the backs of chairs and started poking at small boxes of candy placed at each place setting. A middle-aged man was already digging into the plate of dinner rolls at *our* table and he appeared to have reserved two chairs on either side of him. Something about him was familiar, reminding me of the way I had felt running into Eveline, before I even realized who she was. The middle-aged man stood up once he noticed us approaching.

"Ian," said Mom, pointing to the man, "you remember Mr. Allen, right?"

He smiled and extended his hand. "Hello again," he declared. I shook his hand, which felt rough and swollen. "We met once already, Ian, not sure if you remember that fateful day we all went hiking."

How could I forget?

He smiled and chuckled at his own joke. "Don't call me Mr. Allen. Call me Richard."

Or Dick? "Okay," I answered.

"How's Shannon?" I asked, to be polite, but really I couldn't stop conjuring the image of her slipping the side of her underwear down, showing me her pointed hipbone.

"She's fantastic. She couldn't make it today, though," he said.

That excruciating afternoon with Mr. Allen and Shannon assembled slowly in my mind, a bit like a virus-ridden computer struggling to boot up. Too much had been in my head at the same time that day. Receiving the phone call about Dad's death minutes before we'd left the house had put me in shock and the unpredictable circumstances of our afternoon had left my head spinning.

"Mr. Allen is going to be sitting with us," Mom said.

"Isn't it great to know somebody at one of these things
for once?"

"Really? But who invited him?"

Mom nervously made eye contact with Mr. Allen.
"Actually, Ian, he's *my* guest. I invited him."

"Oh," I said. Now I understood why I had my own seating assignment card that read *no guest* so conspicuously.

Mr. Allen, or Richard, as I had been instructed to call
him, sat on Mom's left while I sat on her right. Mom was
our buffer, our demilitarized zone, and she tried to steer the
conversation so all three of us could socialize together, but
this evolved into Richard and I vying for Mom's attention
by referencing inside stories the other hadn't heard before.
Richard kept trying to insert himself into my stories and I
wanted him to mind his own business and just sit quietly.
I'd only be satisfied if he acted like one of the inanimate
objects at our table—a salt shaker, for instance, or a porcelain creamer. His attempts to be relevant irritated me.

Two other couples joined us. My great-aunt Rebecca
and her husband Paul and a spillover husband and wife
from the bride's side of the family. Once everyone was
seated the banquet waiters dropped fancy salads at each
of our place settings: spinach with goat cheese, tomatoes,
walnuts, and raspberry vinaigrette. Everyone made absurd introductions and caught up on each other's boring
lives between chomping on the dry walnuts.

"Helen, you must introduce me to your handsome
friend?" Aunt Rebecca said to Mom.

"This is Richard Allen," she said, smiling.

Richard nodded at my aunt.

Mom placed her hand on Richard's shoulder and began to massage it.

Creepy.

I grimaced and I wanted Mom to see me do it.

Aunt Rebecca speared a piece of lettuce so large it barely fit on her salad fork. She folded it over and jammed it into her mouth. Then she dabbed globs of vinaigrette from the sides of her mouth with a napkin, leaving the white cloth stained purple, before dropping it haphazardly next to a glass of lemon ice water.

"So, Helen, how did you two meet?" she asked Mom playfully.

Mom blushed, which was something she rarely did. "Wellbourne is a small town. I knew Richard for years, but he reached out to me just when I moved back from Florida. We spent more time together and it just sort of happened. But . . . well . . . it wasn't until recently that we were able to explore other arrangements."

"Yeah, until my father died," I said under my breath.

"What was that, Ian?" asked my aunt.

"Oh, nothing." I smiled.

Mom and Richard were driving me out of my skin, but I took long, deep breaths and told myself to endure it just for one night. I'd survived worse. Clearly, from the beginning Richard had been after more than just Mom's friendship, but she had been a married woman just those short few weeks ago.

"We are so happy," said Mom, leaning her head on Richard's shoulder.

"Helen is perfect," added Richard, gazing into her eyes.

Why couldn't she have told me about this "arrangement" before now? Why did I have to learn about it awkwardly with everyone else? I needed time to mentally prepare.

"Remember that weekend we spent at the Adirondack ski resort, honey? You had the weekend off, remember?" said Richard. "We spent an entire weekend snuggled by the fire? That's when I knew you were the woman for me."

Mom coughed uncomfortably and peeked at me from the corner of her eye.

"Ski resort?" I said. "That sounds like a great time. When was that again?"

I tried to figure out what weekend he was referring to and then what lie she had told about needing to be away.

Richard, who started cutting into his salad, looked up excitedly because I had finally asked him a direct question. "Well, let me see," he said to himself, chewing spiritedly. "Well, it was a month or so after you moved back to Wellbourne? Am I right, Helen?"

Mom shifted in her seat and gently nudged Richard under the table, smiling innocently at me as she did so. "Oh, come on now, Richard," she said nervously. "Ian doesn't want to hear all of the mushy details."

"No, no, I do. This is so very fascinating," I said, laying my chin in my palm.

Mom's expression dropped, but she managed to force a quick smile. "Ian, that's enough," she said, looking around the table nervously. She leaned over and whispered to me: "We can talk about this later. Please don't make a scene."

"Why did you lie to me?" I whispered back.

"What did I lie about?"

"You and Mr. Allen."

"Because it's none of your business, that's why."

"None of my business?"

Without realizing it we had both raised our voices.

"I knew you'd act like this, like you always do," she responded.

"Did you at least tell Dad?" I asked in a normal tone, loud enough for all at the table to hear. "Did you at least tell him before he died?"

"Later, Ian," Mom said between clenched teeth.

Aunt Rebecca, having no sense at first that a grave disagreement was brewing between Mom and me, rested her fork on the corner of her salad plate. I felt sorry for the spillover guests, who'd sat down at table five with no idea why a strange boy and his mother were arguing. They glanced up uncomfortably from their salad plates smeared with raspberry vinaigrette like abstract paintings.

"Who has died?" asked Aunt Rebecca.

Answering calmly Mom said: "Thomas passed away a few—"

"My father," I interrupted. "Thomas Daly. And not one of you said a thing about him tonight."

"I apologize for my prying," Aunt Rebecca replied to Mom, "but I was under the impression Thomas was retired in Florida when you returned. That you two had *separated,* agreeably."

"Is that what you heard?" I fired back. "At least she told you about the split. She told most people that he was finishing up on some *work* down there."

"That's enough, Ian," Mom said, still trying to control the volume of her voice. Her eyes turned red and she bit her lip to stop from crying in front of everyone.

"Oh? And here I thought you two were already divorced," mused Richard. Catching himself, he turned to me. "Ian, are you sure this is the proper time and place?"

"Actually, *Dick*, yes, I do, and if you don't mind, this

is between me and my mother." I turned to her. "It's al-ways how *you* want to see things, Mom. And that's all that matters to you."

Her teary eyes almost made me feel guilty for open-ing my mouth. But I was so angry about everything—the years of deceit, catering to her every whim, the rage she directed at Catherine and me that truly belonged to Dad . . . I had to take a stand now or nothing would ever change. No longer would I cover up and share her ster-ilized version of our reality. The time had come for our so-called family and everyone else in the world to know the truth. Clearly we'd all go home with a metaphorical black eye this night, if that's what it took. All injuries healed in time.

"Is this true, Helen?" asked Aunt Rebecca.

"Well . . . not exactly, I . . ."

"Tell her, Mom," I said. "Tell everybody the truth, we don't need to be ashamed any longer."

Richard pounded his fist on the table. "Now Ian, I have witnessed as much as I can stomach and you will stop this."

Mom peered into her lap and covered her face.

"Are you going to tell them?" I asked.

I didn't look at Richard, who at that moment was probably winding up to knock me out across table five, but Mom simply shook her head no. And anyway, I knew I could slip his punch and knock him right on his ass.

"Screw this," I said, throwing my napkin onto the ta-ble. "I'm out of here."

My knee knocked into the table as I stood and ev-erybody's glasses shook. A wineglass belonging to one of the bride's spillover guests fell over, a thin, delicate stem crashing down into a forest of crisp white linen and polished steel, cracking, bleeding thick red wine onto the centerpiece. Okay, so I made a mess, but I didn't care. I had been concerned with tidiness for far too long.

I marched through the ornate dining room and pushed open a set of glass double doors leading to the grand balcony that overlooked Lake Saguaro. I wanted the doors to slam loudly behind me for dramatic effect, but a mechanism installed at the top ensured they closed with the utmost grace. As angry as I felt, the view of the lake and countryside was soothing, majestic, like some famous landscape painting from a museum. The late-afternoon sun dropped below the mountain range and everything glowed in a radiant light. Soon, after sunset, the shadowed trees, buildings, and the lake itself would all go black.

Decorative lanterns hung from the top of the balcony and lights with bulbs no bigger than loose peas were strung across a black railing, a structure preventing guests who went out for a smoke from careening to the ground fifteen feet below. I sucked in the crisp lake air, letting it roll through me like a refreshing wave. Faraway boats circled the lake, soaking in the last fleeting moments of light, leaving behind streaks of white foam over the water's surface. I heard a soft voice call out from behind me. I knew it couldn't be Mom—though hoped it was her—following me outside to finally apologize and tell me everything from now on would be different.

"Ian? What are you doing out here?"

I glanced over my shoulder to find Eveline standing behind me. She carried a large cardboard box full of clinking bottles, which she set gently on the ground.

"Nothing," I said.

"No fun in there?"

I leaned against the railing and laughed. "No, nothing like that. Sometimes I don't like large groups. What are you doing out here?"

"Out of light beer," she said, pointing to the box. "Thought I'd stock up before the reception *really* gets going."

She joined me at the railing. We hunched over the top as if we were about to spit over the edge. I wondered what her boss would think if he caught her consorting with an unruly guest on the balcony rather than stocking bottles of liquid gold underneath the bar. I scanned both ends of the balcony but we were alone; she was safe, for now, and so was I.

"Try working a bunch of these weddings," she laughed. "They get old real quick."

We watched the remaining flecks of sunlight slip beneath the mountains on the far side of the lake. Mansions, docks, boats, trees, and mountains—everything that I had seen clearly before transformed into one-dimensional black outlines, and then vanished. Even without a clear visual I knew they still existed beyond the void. The balcony where we stood was peaceful, quiet except for the occasional scraping of cutlery on plates from the ballroom. An obnoxious disc jockey started making cliché reception announcements. Nothing could distract me from finally being alone with Eveline. Normally, when I was alone with anyone, I'd search my mind desperately for anything to fill what I perceived as an uncomfortable silence, but on that balcony I was uncharacteristically calm.

"I'm so sorry about that night," I blurted out.

"You're sorry? For what?" she asked.

"I'm just . . . sorry. I should've done something about it earlier, or stuck closer to you."

She let my comment stew before taking a deep breath to respond. "What happened had nothing to do with you, Ian," she said. "I mean, it did later, when you fought Rick. But thanks for saying that. I'm not a kid, Ian, I made my own choices. I thought you didn't like me. I wanted to make you jealous."

Eveline scanned the lake with composure. What I saw in her reminded me of the first time we met. I gave myself permission to truly appreciate how gorgeous she was and accepted that it wouldn't be unthinkable to like her as more than just a friend, but the problem was, I didn't know how to demonstrate my interest. The only "flirting" I had ever seen was in the movies and it seemed outrageous to simply come out and say what was on my mind. Nothing about our exchange felt like it had with Shannon on that mountaintop, when all I cared about was getting off. I couldn't describe the feelings I had for Eveline, because I'd never felt them before.

"You ever get the feeling that you're living in a daydream and all you want to do is wake up?" I asked her. "Sort of like déjà vu?"

"I don't think so," she said. "You?"

"Can I ask you something?" I shuffled my feet on the concrete floor.

"Sure."

"Do you think we ever could've been, you know, at school?"

"*You know*?" She chuckled. "Are you asking if we could've been girlfriend and boyfriend?"

"Yeah, sure." I had always been so certain her answer would've been a resounding no. Our worlds were too far apart. The notion of us actually dating would've been unthinkable. Laughable.

"Sure, why not?" she said.

My heart beat heavily and vibrated across my limbs. "You say that so easily."

"What's wrong with things being easy? Not everything has to be hard," she said, nudging my elbow with hers.

"I've always braced for things to be hard because they always have been, or at least that's what I've believed."

"Hard how?"

"I don't know," I said, pausing for a moment. "Being with you was one of those things I couldn't see happening. I wasn't worthy."

"That's not true!" she said. "Why would you even think like that?"

"It's hard to explain," I said. "I've just been mixed up, but I'm starting to get it together."

She dropped her hand on top of mine, and it was smooth and warm. She commented about how cold my fingers felt. I wanted to stay on the balcony with Eveline forever, under the dreamy lanterns.

"You were the only one, Ian, who acted like a man. You're the only one who ever stood up to that prick. He'd already done that to so many girls, but they were all too ashamed to talk about it."

I didn't know how to respond. I hadn't thought about it that way.

Being heroic wasn't what had led me to the cabin that night, jealousy was. The image of Rick on top of

Eveline drove me to action, but my intention wasn't to make some bold gesture. I had sought to escape with her undetected, then it escalated beyond anything I could've imagined. My other assumption had been that most girls wanted a guy like Rick. He was confident, popular, and a few years older. In many ways he possessed the same traits as my father, which had certainly served him well in his youth. He charmed women—my mother included—into getting whatever he wanted at the time, and then abandoned them to deal with screaming babies, overdue bills, and responsibilities. Men like that only cared about satisfying their own needs by any means possible.

I realized I wasn't like either of them, and I didn't have to be. I wanted to be more.

My decision to help Eveline hadn't been entirely self-less, but in the end I did something good. I had made a choice that night not to fall into the same upside-down world as Rick or my father.

My next steps were unclear and a bit terrifying. I had quite possibly started a chain reaction with Mom.

Thinking about the reception inside, I didn't even know what course was being served or what yarns Mom was spinning to cover up for my deviant behavior. I wondered what they were saying about me in my absence.

My son has always had issues with lying. The boy is unruly. He's like his father.

What a pity about his passing, but I'm happy to see you've moved on.

Sooner or later I'd have to go back inside. I knew that. I could return to the ballroom and pretend nothing had happened—my usual tactic—or I could make everyone understand there was no turning back for me. The cracks couldn't be mended. From that point forward I'd have to fight for every inch of the truth. It wouldn't be easy. I wanted so badly to slide backward, forget all of the silliness of New Brimfield, and be an ignorant little boy again. But I knew too much now. I decided I'd change my way of seeing the world, but it would have to be one step at a time. Meeting the Daly family was the first step and maybe acknowledging my father's death at the Kent & Holbrook Hotel was another. I was certain seeing Eveline again was a step, and an important one. Fate had been arranging it all along.

Eveline pulled a red plastic pen from her back pocket, clicked the top, and carefully wrote down the digits of her new phone number on my hand. "Please call me," she said.

I leaned in and kissed her.

Eveline didn't pull back or appear shocked; she kissed me more deeply. My stress melted away. As long as I took it day by day I knew I could climb out from under the dark cave I'd been living in. Anything was possible. Eveline and I had interlocked our fingers when we kissed and slowly let go of each other's hands so she could return to work. She shuffled over to her box of beer and hoisted it up, hesitating. She used her foot to push open a service door, the box in her hands, and paused to offer me an affectionate smile. I waved and watched the door shut behind her.

Then I turned, glancing through the window at the wedding reception in the ballroom. It seemed like a distant world where I watched but they couldn't see me; they were a movie projected across the spotless window. I was on the outside looking in, but for once it didn't bother me because I was preparing for my new path. The guests were dancing and swinging delicate champagne flutes. The bride and groom suddenly entered to thunderous applause. They were embarking on a new life together. They were celebrating love and honesty, a new beginning, and, most importantly, a prosperous future for themselves and their family.

The End

Acknowledgments

Thank you so much to Kaylie Jones and Johnny Temple for taking a chance on me. My obsession to share this story started over a decade ago, but I first met Kaylie at Wilkes University in 2013. Without her this book wouldn't exist. She understood what I was trying do in the very beginning—before I even knew—and she stuck with me for five years of drafting and revising.

My wife Meghan was both my biggest supporter and critic, which was exactly what I needed. She believed in me every step of the way, through the process of earning my MFA (with all of the new student debt) and working to finalize my manuscript these last three years. During the process we had two beautiful children together, and as cliché as it sounds, they've opened my eyes to a new world.

And thank you to all of the people who have touched this story with their ideas and feedback, including my Kaylie Jones Books readers Lauren Sharkey and J. Patrick Redmond; my close friends John Arkontaky and Brandi Johnson, for giving me a fresh perspective; my Wilkes residency crew Mike Avishai, April Line, and Autumn Whiltshire; and Sara Pritchard, who taught my first fiction class; and the entire Wilkes faculty.